HOW I CHANGED MY LIFE

HOW I CHANGED MY LIFE

By Todd Strasser

SCHOLASTIC INC.

New York Toronto London Auckland Sydney
Mexico City New Delhi Hong Kong Buenos Aires

ISBN 0-439-66105-6

12 11 10 9 8 7 6 5 4 3 2   4 5 6 7 8 9/0

Printed in the U.S.A.   01

First Scholastic printing, May 2004

To my wife, Pamela,
with great love and appreciation

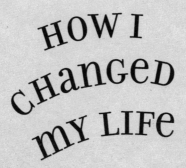

HOW I CHANGED MY LIFE

KYLE

Today I stood up in the front of Pinhead science class and gave an oral report.

"Depending on what sex you are, you either have seven or eight openings in your body," I began.

"All right, Kyle!" Karl Lukowsky stuck his fingers in his mouth and whistled from the back of the room where he'd tilted his chair up against the wall. Karl is thin and gawky with a case of acne that makes his face look like the dark side of the moon. His entire wardrobe consists of four Bart Simpson T-shirts, a couple of pairs of black and white checked pants, and a humongous key ring hanging from his belt.

"That's enough, Karl," said Mr. Orillio, our science teacher.

"The opening I'm going to talk about is the ear," I said.

"Booo!"

"That's enough, Karl."

"It's not one opening, it's two!" yelled Peter Ferrat.

"Hey, Kyle," Jeff Branco shouted. "Didn't Chloe go over your report with you first?"

"Go over it?" Ferrat said. "She usually writes them for him!"

Mr. Orillio told them to shut up, but the Pinheads were on a roll. Mr. Orillio can't be more than five and a half feet tall. His head is so bald it shines. Teachers at my school don't have to wear ties, but he wears one every day. And he always rolls up the sleeves of his shirt to show off his hairy forearms and let everyone know that he may be small, but he's one tough mother of a science teacher.

Crack! Mr. Orillio smacked his yardstick against his desk.

"Either calm down or get sent to the office," he threatened. Then he turned to me. "Continue, Kyle."

"Actually, what I want to talk about is earwax," I said. "Have you ever thought about earwax?"

"No!" several Pinheads shouted and then started to laugh.

Crack! went the yardstick.

"Well, I did," I continued. "I asked myself, where does it come from? What is it for? I mean, the idea that our ears make this stuff is pretty bizarre."

In the back of the room a couple of the Pinheads made snoring sounds.

"Earwax is called cerumen," I said. "It's produced by tiny glands in the ear canal and its job is to keep dust, insects, and other small particles from injuring the inside of the ear."

Lukowsky stuck his finger in his ear and scraped out a glob of brownish-yellow wax.

"Gross!" shouted the Pinheads.

Crack! went the yardstick.

"When we move our jaws to talk or eat, the motion forces the wax upward and out of the ear canal," I said. "When too much wax gathers in the canal, it should be removed by a doctor. Otherwise it can block the canal and impair hearing."

"What'd you say?" Peter Ferrat shouted, and a bunch of Pinheads laughed.

The yardstick went *Crack!*

BO

I spend most of my time on the catwalk in the auditorium. The catwalk is a narrow piece of metal grating about two feet wide that runs about thirty feet above the stage. There are ladders at either end. The techies use the catwalk to hang lights and mikes for stage productions. I use it to hide.

Today Mr. Goodrich stepped onto the stage. Mr. Goodrich is the head of the school drama society. He also teaches honors English, a class I have been known to attend when more attractive alternatives are unavailable. Tall and stooped, with sandy hair that's turning gray, he wears the same yellow cardigan sweater with leather elbow patches every day.

"Bo?" he said, peering up at me.

"Herself," I replied.

"The fall play will be *The Diary of Anne Frank*. We can use some of the props from last spring's production of *Little Women*. I think if you and Bobby do some murals—"

"I can't," I said.

Mr. Goodrich's jaw went slack. "Of course you can, Bo. You've always done it. We'd be lost without you."

I could have suggested that he purchase a compass, or possibly even a sextant. A good road atlas at the very least. But these words I could not utter, for it is not in my nature to be snide.

"I'm sorry," I said.

"I don't understand." Mr. Goodrich looked slightly baffled.

"Chloe Frost."

"So?" Mr. Goodrich pretended to be puzzled, but he understood perfectly. I rested my chin on the catwalk rail and wondered if high school was the same everywhere in the universe—a massive, but unavoidable waste of golden youth.

Mr. Goodrich glanced at the empty auditorium spreading out before us like a huge mouth with 854 upholstered maroon teeth. I think he wanted to make sure Chloe wasn't out there hiding behind a seat and listening.

"Maybe she won't try out," he said in a low voice. "She's already the class treasurer and on the prom planning committee. She might be too busy for the play."

The bell rang. As much as I dreaded mingling

with my fellow detainees, I knew it was time to climb down and attend AP History. Mr. Goodrich waited at the base of the ladder.

"Bo?" Mr. Goodrich went from his desperate look to his helpless look. When I didn't respond, he tried looking like a basset hound puppy that had lost its mother. "Seriously, Bo, I need your help. I believe this will be one of the most important productions I've ever done."

Just between you and me, that wasn't saying much.

KYLE

At the end of the class, Mr. Orillio stood near the door picking his teeth with a toothpick. "Hold up a minute, Kyle."

"Say what?"

"We need to talk."

"Sorry, gotta go," I said.

"Where?"

"Uh, study hall."

Mr. Orillio gave me a "get real" look.

"It's a very important study hall," I said.

"Yeah, right." He smirked. Then he took a pen out of his pocket and turned to a white sheet of paper pinned to the wall next to his collection of "The Far Side" cartoons:

THE FOLLOWING STUDENTS ARE BEING CONSIDERED AS SERIOUS CANDIDATES FOR MR. ORILLIO'S SUMMER SCHOOL SCIENCE SESSION:

Jeff Branco

Peter Ferrat

Under Peter he wrote my name, Kyle Winthrop.

Summer school?

"But I did my report," I protested.

"You had three weeks to do this report," Mr. Orillio said, clicking his pen and putting it back in his pocket. "You didn't want to write it out so I gave you special permission to do it orally. So you copied two paragraphs out of the encyclopedia and read them out loud. They do that in third grade, Kyle."

Out in the hall, groups of kids were pushing toward their next class. I wanted to be out there, lost in the crowd.

"You're not captain of the football team anymore," he said. "It's a new world, pal."

I needed *him* to tell me that?

BO

It isn't easy to compete in a universe populated by the likes of Chloe Frost, who is gorgeous and perpetually tan because she spends every vacation in far-off places where the temperature is always 85 degrees and the ozone layer is virtually nonexistent. She has sand-colored, sun-streaked hair and a model's face with high cheekbones, big brown eyes, a slim nose, and a petite mouth. Her teeth are straight and white, and she has such a perfect body that girls ogle her just as much as boys do.

Chloe and I have been doing school plays since junior high. We never talk. She never attends the cast parties after the shows, probably because she thinks she's above all that. To me, Chloe symbolizes everything that's wrong with our society, everything that's self-centered, hypercompetitive, materialistic, superficial, insincere, and shallow.

Do I sound jealous?

KYLE

Senior lounge is this open space outside the cafeteria with wooden benches along the walls and the sweet sticky smell of lunch in the air. Jeff Branco was stretched out on one of the benches, asleep with his mouth open and the black bandanna he wears on his head pulled down over his eyes. He was wearing a sleeveless black leather motorcycle vest with a hooded gray sweatshirt under it. Timothy Zonin High's very own James Dean.

Chloe was sitting by herself in a corner, bent over a notebook, writing.

I sat down next to her.

"Just a minute," she said, and kept writing. I caught a whiff of perfume and looked at the notebook. Her handwriting is perfect, every letter smooth and flawless as though it was carved by an Olympic figure skater.

"There." She got to the end of the page,

closed the notebook, and put it into the white and blue canvas sailing bag she carries around. It has her initials embroidered in blue: CHF—Chloe Hollow Frost.

"How are you today?" she asked.

"Orillio says I may have to do summer school."

Little creases appeared on her forehead. She hooked her blond hair behind her ear. Three small diamond earrings glinted in her earlobe.

"It was just a warning," I added.

Chloe nodded and reached into her bag and rummaged through all the books she had crammed in there. She picked up a few and put them on my lap. "Hold these a second, Kyle."

On top of the pile was a thin light gray book. *"The Dairy of Anne Frank,"* I read.

"It's *Diary*, silly."

"So it's not about a farmer named Anne, huh?"

"No," Chloe said, taking the books back and putting them in her bag again. "It's the fall play."

"Think you'll be the star?"

Chloe fixed me with her clear brown eyes. "Why do I always have to be the star?"

"I don't know, but you always are."

She pulled a black ledger out of her bag, opened it to a page with a long column of names and numbers on it, and began to add, her slender fingers racing over the keys of the calculator like she was an accountant.

"I just don't know how I'm going to get it all done," she said, more to herself than to me. "Between being the class treasurer, president of SafeRides, head cheerleader, and on the prom planning committee, when am I going to have time to do the play?"

That's what she always says.

BO

Chloe hurt her ankle playing volleyball this afternoon. Nobody actually cares about winning in gym except Chloe, who always must be the best in everything. So while most of the girls were merely pushing the ball back and forth over the net, and praying they wouldn't break a fingernail, Chloe was Ms. Gung Ho. "Come on, you guys, try!" she shouted at us when we started to fall behind the other team. Imagine, if you will, a gaggle of girls wearing baggy maroon shorts and oversized T-shirts who would prefer to be anywhere but gym. And standing in our midst was Chloe, whose T-shirt was practically skin-tight and whose gym shorts were tailored to fit snugly around her perfect tan thighs. She was the only one on our team wearing knee and elbow pads, but then she's the only one who'd ever think of diving for a dig.

"Chill out," snarled Sandra O'Donnell, who's

nearly six feet tall and towers over Chloe. "It's only a game."

"Does that mean you can't try?" Chloe's face was red from exertion. No one else had even broken a sweat.

"It's not important," Sandra said.

"If this isn't important, what is?" Chloe demanded with her hands on her hips.

Sandra rolled her eyes. "Life."

"And this isn't life?" Chloe asked.

"No, it's gym," I said. A couple of girls chuckled, but Chloe pursed her ultraglossy lips and glared at me. I felt myself start to wilt; I'm such a chicken.

"It's so easy to make fun, Bo," she said. "It's so easy to laugh. But I think you're just afraid of what will happen if you try and still lose. Because that would really put a dent in your fragile self-image."

I wished I'd had some clever retort. Maybe something about how I didn't know that Chloe had added psychology to her already prodigious list of abilities. But nothing came to mind, and besides, it didn't matter. Nothing I could say would have fazed her.

"Why don't you all just try for once," she exhorted. "Maybe something truly amazing will happen. Like we might actually win."

Everyone grumbled and groaned and got back into position.

The remarkable thing is, Chloe can be so obnoxious that she actually does get her team to try hard—just so they can get her off their backs. Pretty soon the game was tied, and that was when Chloe leaped up to block Ellen Michner's spike. When she came down, you could hear the "Pop!" as her ankle went out and she crashed to the floor.

The next thing we knew, she was writhing on the ground clutching her ankle and groaning through clenched teeth. Ms. Acevedo, the gym teacher, ran into the office to get an ice pack and the rest of us stood around and watched. Sandra O'Donnell and I glanced at each other and I sensed that she wanted to smile because Chloe had finally gotten what she deserved. But the poor girl really was in pain, and even though we all hated her we were touched by her misery. Ms. Acevedo and two girls helped her to the nurse's office.

I heard she went to the hospital from there.

Perhaps she won't try out for the part of Anne Frank after all.

KYLE

There's a lot of talk about BMs in my house lately. IT's BMs to be precise. IT is my father's one-and-a-half-year-old son. My mother died when I was ten. About four years later my father married this woman named Jackie. She's forty and my father's fifty-two. A year and a half ago, Jackie had IT.

If IT goes three days without a BM, Jackie gets worried. If IT has three bowel movements in one day, Jackie gets nervous. If IT's BMs smell bad, Jackie wants to know why. Likewise if they smell good.

Tonight IT had a BM that didn't smell at all. I was sitting in the den watching college ball on TV. My father was in the kitchen. From the stairs I heard Jackie say, "Brian, could you come here?" in that nervous tone of voice that always gets my father's attention. He went upstairs to the nursery.

"What's the problem?" I heard him ask.

"Smell this," Jackie said.

"That?" I bet my father was thrilled.

"Please, Brian."

I can just see my father bending over and taking a whiff.

"So?" I heard my father say.

"It doesn't smell," Jackie said.

"Well, that's great."

"It's not normal," Jackie insisted. "A baby's BMs should smell."

"Maybe it depends on what he eats," my father said.

"Do you think I should call Dr. Huber?" Jackie probably calls the pediatrician five times a day.

"Let's wait a day and see what happens," my father said. That's his standard reply. On the way back downstairs he stopped in the den.

"A BM that didn't smell." I winked.

"Yeah." He smiled slightly. "Be nice if we could patent it. So who's playing?"

"Syracuse and Georgetown. Third quarter. The Hoyas are up by six."

"Homework all done?"

The Hoyas' quarterback stepped into the pocket and hit the tight end for a fourteen-yard gain. My father stood in the doorway and waited for my answer. When it didn't come, he said,

"Come on, Kyle, it's senior year. Just get through it. You're going to need that diploma."

I stared at the TV, and my father stared at me. It was like he wanted to say something more, but it had all been said before.

BO

I know it's wrong to delight in other people's misfortunes, but Chloe's the kind of person who makes you want to break that rule. It's not just that she's so obnoxious. What truly galls me is that she doesn't seem to care whether we like her or not. And she's so . . . *perfect*. (Her father is a plastic surgeon. Maybe he created her in his laboratory.) If I looked like her, I really think I'd be content . . . just to be me.

KYLE

I wheeled Chloe to the audition for that play today. Half a dozen people were sitting in the auditorium when we got there. Everyone started to whisper as I pushed Chloe down the aisle.

Mr. Goodrich was up on the stage, holding a clipboard. He teaches Pinhead English and we always give him a hard time.

"Why, Chloe." He looked surprised. "What are you doing here?"

"I'm going to audition," Chloe said as I helped her onto the stage.

"In your condition?" Mr. Goodrich frowned. I got the feeling he wasn't too thrilled.

"I'll be walking in a few days," Chloe said.

"Well, er, I see." Mr. Goodrich wasn't doing a great job of hiding his disappointment. "I suppose you want to be Anne."

Chloe responded by reciting by heart about five minutes worth of lines from the play.

Everyone in the auditorium became silent.

"Uh, that was very impressive, Chloe," Mr. Goodrich said when she was finished. He turned and looked out at the kids sitting in the audience. "Does anyone else want to try out for the part of Anne Frank?"

No one said a word.

"Now come on," Mr. Goodrich said. "I know several of you said you were going to."

"That was before Chloe," this voice said from above us.

I looked up and saw two girls and a guy with long blond dreadlocks sitting on the catwalk above the stage.

"I assure you I'll be absolutely fair in my decision, Bo," Mr. Goodrich said.

"That's what they're afraid of," the girl said. She was wearing black jeans and a blue plaid shirt. Her long, thick brown hair was pulled back in a ponytail. I knew her because she sometimes baby-sat for IT.

Mr. Goodrich sighed and looked down at his clipboard. "All right. That ends the audition for Anne. Next we need an able-bodied male for the part of Peter Van Daan. Any volunteers?"

No one volunteered. I noticed that there weren't many guys in the audience. Mr. Goodrich turned and looked at me. "How about you, Kyle?"

"Me?" Act in a school play?

"No," said Chloe.

I was surprised she'd answered for me. Mr. Goodrich looked surprised, too.

"I, uh, just don't think it's a good idea," Chloe sort of stammered.

"Shouldn't that be Kyle's decision?" Mr. Goodrich asked.

"Kyle . . . " Chloe had this pained look on her face. It was pretty obvious she didn't want me to do it.

"Guess not, Mr. G," I said.

BO

I was sitting on the catwalk with my dear friends
Alice Hacket and Bobby Shriner. Alice is five feet
four inches, has short black hair and the palest
skin imaginable, which she accents by wearing
thick black mascara and deep red lipstick.
Someday she's either going to be a vampire or a
great character actress. Bobby is six feet tall and
must weigh ninety pounds. He has deep blue eyes
and long blond dreadlocks that are the envy of
every girl in school. He's a fabulous artist and
someday he's going to be a world-renowned set
designer.

It's wonderful to have friends who are going
to be famous.

We were waiting for the audition to begin
when Chloe made a grand entrance in her
wheelchair, propelled by her ever-present
attendant/paramour—the former captain of the

football team and a hunk of major crush proportions named Kyle Winthrop.

"I thought you said she wasn't trying out," Alice whispered as if it was my fault Chloe had chosen to tread in the holy sanctuary of the auditorium.

"I didn't think she would," I whispered back. "But don't worry. You're a much better actress."

"According to whom?"

"Everyone."

Alice rolled her mascaraed eyes toward the ceiling, which was only a few feet away. Then she crossed her arms unhappily. We watched Kyle lift Chloe out of the wheelchair and place her ever so gently on the stage.

"Didn't he hurt his knee last year?" Alice whispered.

"I heard they had to completely reconstruct it," whispered Bobby. "They say he can never play sports again."

Kyle picked up the wheelchair and put it on the stage. Then he climbed up and helped Chloe back into it.

"Such a gent," I said with a wistful sigh. "The head cheerleader and the captain of the football team. . . . It's as American as capital punishment."

"I always wondered what those two saw in each other," Alice whispered. "I mean, Chloe's practically the class valedictorian. Isn't Kyle sort of dumb?"

"No," Bobby said. "He and I used to be in the resource room together, like when we were in elementary school."

"*You* were in the resource room?" Alice asked, surprised.

"Forever," Bobby said. "And I had a reading tutor twice a week."

"But you love to read," I said.

"Now," said Bobby. "I had no choice. I *had* to learn to read to survive."

"What about Kyle?" Alice asked.

"Kyle had sports."

KYLE

Skipped math and went down to the senior lounge. Eddie Lampel was there, decked out in prepster khakis and a blue oxford shirt. Eddie's the first string quarterback and probably my best bud at school.

"Yo, bro." We slapped high fives and I slid down next to him on the bench.

"How's the knee?" he asked.

"Still attached."

"Swelling?"

"Not bad. Had it drained last week."

"Bummer." Eddie shook his head. "But, hey, no sense in being crippled for the rest of your life, right?"

"Right." It was bull and Eddie and I both knew it. It killed me not to be on the team anymore.

"How's the scholarship scene?" I asked.

"Lookin' good, bro. Couple of scouts comin'

to the game Saturday. Schools callin' the house. I …" Eddie caught himself. "Aw, maybe I shouldn't talk about it."

"Naw, it's okay."

"What a pisser, man. It was gonna be you and me. We were gonna bite the big enchilada, right? Get those four-year rides, meet in the Rose Bowl someday."

For a second we were both lost in the vision of 100,000 screaming fans cheering us on that warm New Year's day in Arizona that would never be. Then Eddie started to chew the skin on the side of his thumb. I could tell there was something else on his mind.

"What's up?"

"Coach Cicippio wants me to ask you about something. I told him you'd never go for it, but he made me promise I'd ask anyway."

"Sorry, Eddie, I've already got a date for the prom."

Eddie grinned for a second. "I just want you to know this was his idea, not mine."

"Okay, okay. The suspense is killing me."

"He wants to know if you want to be the equipment manager."

I stared at him in total disbelief. *"The dweeb?"*

"I told him you'd never do it."

I didn't know what to say. The dweeb is always some loser too small or uncoordinated to play ball. So he gets the job of keeping track of the team's equipment and hauling it around to games.

"I think Cicippio was just trying to figure out a way you could be with the team," Eddie said. "So you could still be part of it."

"Yeah."

We sat there for a few moments without saying anything more. Then Eddie got up. "Gotta skate, bro."

So I sat there alone, in a state of semishock. The dweeb, I kept thinking. Was that all I was good for anymore?

BO

I read *The Diary of Anne Frank* tonight. It's so sad. You almost wish it wasn't a true story, and that she really didn't have to hide in an attic to escape the Nazis during World War II. At a time when she should have been outside playing and having fun with her friends, she had to spend day and night cooped up in a small room with her parents and assorted other peculiar people, almost none of whom she got along with.

The one thing I found truly difficult to understand was how she managed to remain cheerful and hopeful in such a miserable situation. Even at the end, after the Nazis found her and she was about to be sent to a concentration camp, she wrote, "In spite of everything, I still believe that people are really good at heart."

I think if she'd gone to the same elementary school I attended, her outlook would have been different.

KYLE

They had a career fair in the gym today. Chloe said you could walk around and talk to people about careers in the health profession and accounting and sales and so forth. She said there's going to be a couple of career days this fall. Like Time Zone High has finally figured out that they better prepare us for something before it's too late.

Of course, being Persons In Need of Supervison, the PINS got sent to the library instead. It's not that the Pinheads are dummies. It's just that most of us have "demonstrated an inability to behave responsibly in an unstructured environment." In other words, we tend to screw up. In the library we usually just sit around and look at magazines, but today I went over to the desk where Ms. Shepard, the librarian, works.

"Can I help you, Kyle?" she asked.

"I'm looking for a book," I said.

"Then you've come to the right place." Ms. Shepard winked. She's okay. I mean, at least she doesn't act afraid of us the way some teachers do.

So she found the book of Anne Frank's diary. Then we figured out that what I really wanted was the play. She found that, too. Then she had us get in a circle and talk about careers. Like on the off chance one of us actually has a goal in life.

"Do any of you think about a career?" she asked.

Lukowsky raised his hand, so you knew the answer was going to be perverted. "I wanna own an adult video store," he said, and displayed his dumb toothy grin.

"So what else is new?" Ms. Shepard asked, and everyone laughed.

Then Jeff Branco raised his hand.

"What kind of career are you interested in, Jeff?" Ms. Shepard asked.

"A career in crime," said Jeff. That cracked everyone up.

"I'm serious," said Ms. Shepard.

"So am I," Jeff said. "If you just do burglaries and stuff, you can do okay."

"You'll go to jail," said Ms. Shepard.

"Naw, the first couple of times you get caught they just slap your wrist and let you go," Jeff said. "Then when they figure out you're a repeat offender, you'll do a few months in the slammer, but you always get out early 'cause they need the cells for the really violent criminals."

"How do you know that?" Ms. Shepard asked.

"My Uncle Benny," said Jeff.

"How does he know?"

"He's a crook."

Way to go, Jeff.

BO

My full Christian name is Bolita Helena Chatsworth Vine. Is that a name or a curse? Still, I'd rather have people address me by my full first name than what most of them do call me, which is Bo. Bo Vine. That's right, as in cows.

In ninth grade the school psychologist told me I had poor communication skills. If that's true, I must've inherited them from my mother. Instead of speaking to me, she leaves articles from newspapers and magazines in my room. I would estimate that close to 90 percent of the articles concern weight loss and/or having a positive self-image.

Every week nearly six thousand children around the world die of disease and malnutrition. We are poisoning our environment, and millions of people are homeless. All my mother can think about is cellulite. Then again, what would you expect from a woman who named her only child Bolita?

A lot of my self-image has to do with the school theater. If it wasn't for the theater, I'd probably be a bag woman. All I live for is the next production. When you're working on a play, you're in a different world. The only thing that matters is putting on the most fabulous performance possible. I admit it's an escape. But have you ever noticed that escape always involves going from something undesirable to something desirable? We escape from fires, or jail, or go on a vacation escape.

What's so bad about that? Nothing as far as I can see. Except that how can I escape if I'm not going to do *The Diary of Anne Frank*?

KYLE

I came out of the lunch line and headed toward the football table, where all the guys from the team sit. To get there, you have to walk past the Pinhead table. I guess I've walked past it for years.

"Hey, Kyle!" Peter Ferrat waved at me. Peter's a little guy with dark hair and a big pointy nose. Everyone calls him the Rat. He was sitting with the other PINS, and they were all looking at me.

"What?"

"How come you never sit with us?" Peter asked.

"I sit with the team," I told him.

"Yeah, but you're not on the team anymore."

I just stared at him for a second, then headed over to the guys and sat down next to Eddie. Alex Gidden and Jason Rooney, the two defensive ends, were there.

"What'd the Rat want?" Jason asked.

"Wanted to know why I never sit with them."

"Sit with those dirtbags?" Alex sneered. "Get real."

"They're not so bad," I said.

"Lukowsky's a pervert," Jason muttered smugly.

That kind of pissed me off. Not that it isn't true, but Jason doesn't even *know* the guy.

BO

Bobby and I talked today while we made the rounds with the recycling wagon. Picking up recyclable paper in the classrooms is one of the few activities for which I will voluntarily leave the catwalk. Bobby's so gorgeous. But at ninety pounds, there just isn't enough of him. He's not only an incredible artist and set designer. He's also one of the most perceptive people I know.

"You can't not do *Anne Frank*, you know," he said, gazing at me through his beautiful blond dreadlocks.

"How can you say that?" I said.

"I know you. Without the theater you're lost. Like a virgin without a sacrifice."

"Aren't we getting a little personal?" I asked as we emptied the blue recycling crate in Mrs. Porter's room.

Bobby just smiled, revealing his brilliant white teeth. I've never talked about sex with him.

He just *knows* things like that.

"You can't go through life letting people like Chloe stop you from doing what you really want to do."

"But she's so obnoxious."

"I don't find her obnoxious," Bobby said.

"You don't have to play volleyball with her."

"You think she's obnoxious just because she wants to win all the time?" Bobby asked. "She's a perfectionist, Bo."

"Since when does *she* get to dictate what our collective vision of perfection should be?" I asked.

"She doesn't," Bobby replied. "She's just one of many people who contribute to that vision."

"Well, if you ask me, she contributes a lot more than her share," I said.

"If you give up the theater because of Chloe, you're just cutting off your nose to spite your face."

"Who's going to stage-manage?" I asked.

Bobby straightened up and brushed the blond hair out of his blue eyes. "Is that what this is about? Making everyone realize how valuable you are? Are you waiting for us all to come crawling on our knees begging?"

"Not you and Alice." I grinned. "But everyone else would be nice."

KYLE

TV sports gets a little dicey on weekday after-noons. Volleyball's pretty cool. It's fast and they make some amazing digs, but it's not on the tube that often.

Today I watched Hovercraft racing from England, but it was completely bogus. They float around a grass track like bumper cars, except every once in a while one of them flips over. After a while I got bored. Then I remembered I'd brought home that *Anne Frank* play.

I've always had a hard time concentrating when I read. When I was younger, I had to have a lot of help at school, like in the resource room and stuff like that. Then I got into sports and people would say things like, "Thank God Kyle's got football."

Today it was doubly difficult to read because IT is teething. That means he staggers around the house screaming and drooling while Jackie runs after him trying to rub pink junk into his gums.

I was staring at the cover of the play when the door to my room opened and IT waddled in pulling a wooden train on a string.

"Wha dis?" he asked, holding up the train.

"A boat," I said.

"Bo, bo." IT waddled back out. Of course I had to get up and close the door again.

I kind of skimmed through the play. Surprise, surprise: Peter is sort of Anne's boyfriend. Now why do you think Chloe wouldn't want me to have that part?

BO

Every so often I baby-sit for Jake Winthrop, the child of Jackie and Brian Winthrop. Brian is also the father, by his first marriage, of Kyle Winthrop, who is the Kyle in Kyle and Chloe. Jake is an adorable little boy, except he gets the names of things mixed up. The other night he kept pointing at a box of Ritz crackers and saying "Soap, soap." He also calls trains boats and soda milk.

When I baby-sit for the Winthrops on Saturday nights, Kyle is usually gone before I arrive and I assume he returns after I've left. When I do run into him, he will most likely nod and say hello. I will most often nod and say hello back. I believe he knows who I am, but I'm not certain he knows I exist.

There was a time when I was intimidated by people like Kyle Winthrop and Chloe Frost. They seemed so popular and special that I questioned why they would want to talk to me. But recently (and perhaps because of all those articles my mother leaves on my dresser) I've begun to wonder why I should have such a poor self-image. I'm a nice person, a good person, a smart person. Besides, we're all just human beings, granted equal rights under the constitution and in the eyes of the law, etc. It has occurred to me of late that if a Chloe Frost or a Kyle Winthrop were ever to refuse to talk to me, I could make a strong case arguing that they were the jerks, not me.

Anyway, I baby-sat for Jake last Saturday and when I arrived, Kyle was just going out. We met at the front closet where I was taking off my jacket. Kyle's shirt and slacks looked pressed and neat, so it was obvious he was going out with Chloe.

Kyle is tall and broad-shouldered and very handsome in an all-American, square-jawed kind of way. Despite everything I just said about improving my self-image, my immediate reaction was to be completely overcome by an acute case of tingly girlish nervousness, and to grow totally silent for fear of saying anything that might cause him to think I was a complete bozo. Of course, nothing would make him think I was a complete bozo faster than if I just stood there and didn't say anything.

So I said, "Hi."

"Hi," he said and stood there in the hallway

waiting for me to hang up my jacket.

Normally, I would have quickly hung up my jacket and then hurried down the hall pretending that Jackie was in desperate need of help with Jake. At best, while hanging up my jacket, I might have tried to think of something intelligent to say and of course rejected every idea I came up with, and then hurried down the hall. Finally, I would have spent the rest of the night in self-flagellation for being such a chicken and not saying anything to Kyle.

But something different happened last Saturday.

I hung up my jacket.

I turned to hurry down the hall.

But then I stopped and looked up. Kyle's eyes met mine. His were deep blue and mesmerizing. I felt like I was in a trance, but I knew if I didn't say something I'd look like an idiot just staring at him like that.

So I said, "How's your knee?"

He blinked and said, "Not so great, I guess."

"Will you ever be able to play football again?"

"It's probably not a good idea."

"You must be really disappointed," I said. Inside, I felt like I was on a bobsled hurtling down the side of a mountain, barely able to steer and completely unable to stop. It felt both terrifying and thrilling. *I was talking to Kyle Winthrop!*

And he wasn't acting like I was a total boob. In fact, Kyle was studying my face with astonishment, as if I'd just made some wildly brilliant deduction. "Yeah, actually I am."

"That's too bad," I said. "I'm sorry."

I could tell by the way Kyle looked at me that this may have been the first time he ever registered me as a human being. So then I did the oddest thing. I reached into the closet and said, "Denim or leather?"

Kyle gave me a blank look for a moment. Then he said, "Uh, what's it like out?"

"It's not bad," I said. "May I suggest denim?"

"Sure."

I handed him his denim jacket.

"Bo?" Jackie called from Jake's room. "Can you come here?"

"Okay," I called back and then turned to Kyle. "Guess I have to go to work. See ya."

"Yeah," said Kyle.

I went down the hall without looking back. It took every ounce of will power not to break into a joyous skip or burst out in triumphant, hysterical laughter. I even giddily imagined him standing there, staring at my back, thinking, *Who was that incredibly intelligent and sensitive young woman?* and *How have I lived this long without getting to know her better?*

Well, *that* may have been stretching things.

As soon as everyone was out of the house, I called Alice.

"You won't believe this," I said. "You know Kyle Winthrop, Chloe's boyfriend?"

"Never heard of him," Alice deadpanned.

"The funniest thing just happened," I said. Then I told her about Kyle and me and the closet. "And what I found so amazing was that while I was nervous, it wasn't that awful I-really-hate-this-and-wish-I-would-die kind of nervousness! It was a wonderful this-is-fabulous-and-really-exciting kind of nervousness!"

"Amazing," Alice said unenthusiastically.

"Well, I think it is," I said.

"That you talked to Kyle Winthrop?"

"That we communicated. That we related. That I got him his jacket."

Alice was quiet for a moment. Then she said, "Want to know what I think?"

"Yes."

"I think you're coming unglued, Bo," Alice said.

KYLE

We were sitting on the couch in Chloe's house watching MTV on her father's giant screen TV. Her foot was still bandaged and she had it propped up under a couple of pillows.

"I took that play, *Anne Frank*, out of the library," I said.

Chloe's head turned slowly until she was facing me. It was like she didn't want to rush it because she was collecting her thoughts and wanted to know exactly what she was going to say when we were face to face.

"Why?"

"Just curious."

"You've never read one of our plays before."

"I wanted to see the part this guy Peter has," I explained.

Like a high punt, the words hung in the air between us for two, three, four seconds. . . .

"I don't understand," Chloe finally said.

"Well, now that I'm off the team, I've got all this free time."

Chloe is not a relaxed person. She almost *never* relaxes. But after I told her this, I swear she grew twice as tense as normal. Instead of saying anything more, she turned back to the TV.

"So guess what?" I said.

"What, Kyle?"

"Turns out this guy Peter is Anne's boyfriend."

"Barely."

"How come you didn't want me to play that part?" I asked.

Chloe didn't answer. She wouldn't even look at me. I could see it wouldn't do any good to upset her, so I changed the subject.

"Why don't we get out of here for a while?" I asked, sliding a little closer to her on the couch.

Chloe didn't budge. "Dr. Honigman said the more I'm off my ankle, the faster it will heal."

"You'll just be in the car."

"Cruising?" Chloe made a face like she was sucking on a lemon.

"We could park."

"You know how I hate that." Chloe crossed her arms in front of her.

"Well, we could fool around here."

"I'll never do that again."

Right. One night last year, Chloe and I were

messing around on the couch and her parents came in *with another couple*. We weren't even doing anything serious, but it was still incredibly embarrassing, especially for Chloe, who really hates to be caught off-guard doing anything.

Of course there was my house, but even though my father and Jackie were out, the baby-sitter was still there with IT.

So that meant we were stuck at Chloe's watching the tube all night. Somehow, I wasn't surprised.

BO

"Don't try to be who you're not." You've probably heard that saying. But the question is, who are we? And who decides who we are? A good actor becomes the character he's playing. Why stop when the performance is over?

❖ ❖ ❖

I was hiding on the catwalk, minding my own business, when I heard footsteps on the stage below. Looking down I saw Mr. Goodrich.

"You're looking well, Bo."

"Thanks, but flattery will get you nowhere."

"I mean it. You've lost weight, haven't you?"

I was secretly delighted that someone had noticed, but I wasn't about to succumb to sweet nothings. "Let's cut to the chase, Mr. G."

Mr. Goodrich slid his hands into his pockets. "Chloe is going to be Anne."

"How can the lead be played by someone in a

wheelchair with a cast from her hip to her ankle?"
I asked.

"Don't exaggerate. She's only wearing an Ace bandage and walking with a cane."

"I thought she was still supposed to be on crutches this week," I said.

"She's made an unusually fast recovery."

"Figures."

"You have to stage-manage this production," Mr. Goodrich said.

"Isn't it time you found someone new?" I asked. "What are you going to do next year when I'm gone?"

"I'll . . ." Mr. Goodrich hesitated. "I'll worry about it then."

"Tsk, tsk." I wagged a finger at him. "Short term planning."

"Just say yes, Bo."

I took a dramatic pause. "I can't, Mr. G. I can't take her prima donna attitude, and I can't stand the way she manipulates you and everyone else in the cast."

"Chloe doesn't manipulate me."

"Then why has she had the lead role in every play for the past three years?" I asked.

"Because she's a fine young actress and she deserves it."

"Alice Hacket can act circles around Chloe, and you know it."

"If the right play came along, I'm sure Alice would have the lead," Mr. Goodrich said.

"If the right play came along?" I repeated in disbelief. "It's not like these things are left up to chance, Mr. G. You choose the plays."

Mr. Goodrich got stern. "Now listen to me, Bo, you are the best stage manager I have."

Mr. Goodrich is so cute when he tries to be firm. But he'd probably make more of an impression if his lower lip didn't quiver so much.

"No," I said.

And then it happened. Another person stepped onto the stage. I looked down and saw the top of Kyle Winthrop's head.

Kyle stopped about ten feet from Mr. Goodrich. He glanced up at me on the catwalk.

"Didn't mean to interrupt," he said.

"Not at all, Kyle," Mr. Goodrich said. "What's up?"

Kyle cleared his throat. "Uh, I was just wondering about the part of Peter in *The Diary of Anne Frank*."

"What about it?" Mr. Goodrich asked.

"Is it still available?" Kyle asked.

Mr. Goodrich looked up at me. The expression on his face said, "Is this a joke?"

"Forgive me for asking, Kyle," Mr. Goodrich said, "but have you ever acted before?"

"Is it a problem if I haven't?" Kyle asked.

I knew what Mr. Goodrich was thinking: The role of Peter could basically be played by a cardboard cutout. In fact, it probably would be if he didn't find a willing male soon.

"You've got the part," Mr. Goodrich said.

Kyle looked surprised. "Uh, well, I uh . . . I'm not really sure I want it. I mean, I was just wondering. I really have to think about it, okay?"

"Fine, Kyle," Mr. Goodrich said. "But try to let me know soon or I may have to give the part to someone else."

"Okay, sure," Kyle said. Then he waved at me. For some reason, nearly everyone waves at me when I'm thirty feet above them. "Uh, see ya." He left the stage.

I gave Mr. Goodrich an incredulous look. "Give the part to someone else?"

He responded with a wink. "I was just trying to sell him on it, Bo."

KYLE

In the student lounge today Chloe poked her finger into my stomach. "What's this?"

"Uh, last night's pizza with mushrooms and sausage?"

"I'm serious," she said.

"So am I."

"You're not going to get fat, are you?" she asked.

"Wasn't planning on it."

"Nobody plans to get fat," she said.

The conversation sort of ground to a halt. That seems to happen a lot lately. Used to be she and I could talk for hours about the team, the games, what parties we were going to . . . I mean, it wasn't earth-shattering stuff, but it was what we had in common. Now, I don't know. It feels like something's missing.

Chloe reached down into her bag and took out her gray copy of *Anne Frank*. I watched over her shoulder. She'd highlighted all of her lines in yellow and she moved her lips as she read and made little gestures with her head and shoulders, as if acting out the words. Naw, I thought, I couldn't do it. I couldn't memorize all those lines. I couldn't get up on the stage in front of everyone and act. It was a dumb idea.

BO

Two or three times a week I swim. Except for me, hardly anyone under the age of twenty-five uses the junior high pool at night. I can go there with a reasonable amount of certainty that I won't be seen.

Last night I was leaving the house when my mother came in carrying two plastic shopping bags filled with groceries.

"Swimming again?" she asked, setting the bags on the kitchen table.

"No, I'm just taking my towel for a walk."

My mother gave me a weary look. "Why do you always have to be this way?"

"It's the age," I said.

"This is the fourth night in a row you've gone swimming," she said as she started to put away the groceries. "Usually you're gone for forty-five minutes. Lately you've been going for an hour and a half."

I was surprised that she'd been keeping track. Then she pulled a familiar looking ice-cream container out of one of the shopping bags.

"Not Ben & Jerry's Monster Mash!" I gasped.

"I thought you liked it," she said.

"I love it," I said. "That's the problem."

"What's the problem?"

"Mom. Look at me for God's sake."

She squinted at me. "You don't look well."

"What are you talking about? I've lost five pounds."

"Why?"

"I don't know. I just felt like it."

"Are you sure you're not sick?"

"Mom, I feel great. I swear, I've never felt better."

"You've never wanted to lose weight before," my mother said.

"People change," I said.

My mother studied me with a somewhat bewildered look on her face. I've always wished someone would think of me as exotic and mysterious. I just wish it wasn't my mother.

❖ ❖ ❖

I wear goggles to keep the chlorine out of my eyes when I swim. They always fog up so badly that I can hardly see anything except the heavy black lane lines painted on the bottom of the pool. Until recently I swam at a leisurely pace and never pushed myself. The water was my friend. It was there to soothe and give temporary relief from the harsh realities of the world at large. Lately I've been swimming harder and longer. The water has become my ally in the war against liposomes.

At some point in my swim I noticed that someone was doing laps in the lane next to mine, but I didn't think much about it. Lots of people swim at night, but I rarely look at them.

Later, after I finished my last lap in a blinding burst of Olympic-record speed, I hung onto the edge of the pool and caught my breath. That's when I noticed that the swimmer in the lane next to mine had also stopped. Of course, with my swimming goggles still on he was just a big foggy blur.

"I'm impressed," he said.

"Why?" I asked without my usual girlish nervousness. After all, I didn't feel like I was talking to a guy. I felt like I was talking to a blur.

He said something, but I couldn't hear clearly because my ears were full of water. I asked him to repeat it.

"You swam a lot of laps," he said.

"I wasn't counting."

"You come here a lot?" he asked.

That's when I noticed something familiar about his voice. I pulled off my goggles and gasped. "Oh, my God!"

"What's wrong?" Kyle asked. He was bobbing in the lane next to me with his black hair plastered down on his head.

"It's you."

"So?"

"Well, I . . ." I stammered. "I had these goggles on and my ears are filled with water."

"You thought I was someone else?" Kyle asked.

"I just didn't know," I said. My heart had started beating so hard I expected to see little waves rippling away from my body. "When did you start swimming here?"

"My first time."

The pool drains made gurgling sounds. I felt like my heart was starting to slow down. I had to get calm. I had to stop acting like a total bozo.

"You just felt like swimming?" I asked.

"Doctor says this puts the least strain on my knee."

I could think of no appropriate response. Normally, my nervousness would have made me get out of the water, pronto, but I was reluctant to let Kyle see me wet and fat. So I tried to think of something to say. And that's when I remembered the play.

"Did you make up your mind?" I asked.

"Huh?"

"About the play."

"Oh, yeah, I don't think so," he said.

I was surprised by the enormity of the disappointment I suddenly felt. Why did I care? But as I floated in the chilly water, clearly in danger of succumbing to hypothermia, I realized I did care.

"Can I ask why not?"

"Guess I just realized it wasn't a good idea."

"You probably imagined what it must feel like to stand up in front of four hundred people and blow your lines."

"Well, that doesn't bother me," Kyle said.

"It doesn't?" I was surprised.

"You know how many times I've stood up in front of eight hundred people and dropped an easy interception?" he asked.

"No."

"Plenty. You get used to it."

"Then what's the difference?"

"I may have blown the catch, but at least I knew what I was doing."

"This is a high school play," I said. "You don't have to know what you're doing."

Kyle grinned. I would have grinned back, but then Kyle would have noticed that my teeth were chattering. He still appeared to be in no rush to go. Meanwhile, I'd been in the water for so long I felt like I was going to turn into a blue prune.

"Anyway, Mr. G has probably given the part to someone else by now," Kyle said.

"There is no one else," I said. "He was just trying to stampede you into a decision."

"Serious?"

"Uh-huh."

Kyle studied me for a moment. "Do you think I should do it?"

I pictured Chloe bossing everyone around and being her usual prima donna self . . . and Kyle being there to see it all.

"Well, if you really want my opinion," I said, "I think you should."

Kyle didn't really react. I couldn't tell if my answer meant anything to him or not, and I couldn't wait around any longer to find out.

"I'd love to stay and talk to you, but I'm starting to freeze to death," I said.

"You mean that isn't blue lipstick?" Kyle asked playfully.

"Very funny." I gave him a cute smile and climbed out of the pool, quickly pulling a towel around me. When I turned, Kyle gave me a slight wave.

At least he wasn't throwing up.

❖ ❖ ❖

Later I had a burst of inspiration and called Alice. Last year she started subscribing to a computer bulletin board, and she tends to fall in and out of love with other hackers at an alarming rate.

When she answered, she was crying. "It's over, Bo."

"Excuse me?"

"A college student I met on-line," she explained.

"You didn't tell me about him."

"I didn't have time," Alice said. "It happened so quickly."

"Maybe you should try having a relationship with someone in person."

"Easier said than done, Bo. So what's up?"

"Can you use this fabulous computer service of yours to find out how many former football players went on to become actors?"

"Easy," Alice said. I heard the plastic tapping of computer keys. "There's a sports RTC almost every night."

"A what?"

"Real time conference," Alice said. "Get a piece of paper."

I grabbed a paper bag from the garbage and a brand-new eyebrow pencil while Alice typed in the question and started getting answers.

"Joe Namath, Brian Bosworth, Jim Brown, John Matuzak, Ed Marinaro, Alex Karras, and Bubba Smith. What's this for, anyway?"

"Hold it," I gasped, scribbling furiously on the bag. "Okay, got 'em. That's amazing."

"Just a pit stop on the information super-highway."

"Well, thanks," I said. "Gotta go."

I hung up and called the Winthrops' house. Jackie answered and I asked to speak to Kyle.

"Hello?"

"Hi, it's Bolita Vine."

"Huh . . . ?"

"From the pool tonight."

"Oh, Bo. What's up?"

"What do Brian Bosworth, Jim Brown, Joe Namath, Ed Marinaro, Bubba Smith, Alex Karras, and John Matushuk all have in common?"

"It's Matuzak," Kyle corrected me.

"Okay, okay."

"Let's see. Matuzak was a defensive tackle and Bosworth was a middle linebacker. Namath was a QB. Brown was a running back. Namath had the knee. I don't think Bosworth was ever on a Super Bowl winning team . . ."

"They were all football players who became actors," I said.

"Hey, that's right."

"So if you decide to play Peter, you won't be alone."

Kyle was quiet for a moment. Then he said, "You *really* think I should do it?"

I felt a thrill rush through me. Kyle Winthrop

was asking my opinion about something, and he sounded sincere!

"Yes," I said. "I really think you should."

KYLE

Welcome to Pinhead English. Today Mr. Goodrich wanted to talk about this book called *The Outsiders* we were supposed to read over the summer.

"Did anybody read it?" he asked.

I looked around the room. The only kid who raised his hand was the Rat. But he was probably lying. Mr. Goodrich took off his glasses and rubbed his forehead. He does that when he's ticked off.

"This was the only assignment you had all summer," he said. "Why couldn't you do it?"

"Cause there were no sex scenes," Lukowsky said.

"Thank you for that insightful reply," Mr. Goodrich said.

"I'm serious," said Lukowsky. "You want us to read, right? How about giving us something we'll like."

"I think the school's position is that if you want to read pornography, you can find it on your own," Mr. Goodrich said.

"He's not talking about porn, you dork," Jeff Branco said.

"Watch your mouth or you'll be paying a visit to Mr. Rope," Mr. Goodrich warned.

"Wimp," Branco muttered.

"What?" Mr. Goodrich said.

"Nothing." It was obvious that Jeff was peeved about something.

"I'm not talking about porn," Lukowsky said.

"Then what *are* you talking about?" Mr. Goodrich snapped impatiently.

"Uh-oh, watch it," someone whispered. "He's getting pissed."

"I'm talking about *books* with sex scenes," Lukowsky said. "I mean, books are supposed to be about life, right? Well, sex is part of life."

"Not part of *your* life, Zitface," Jeff Branco said.

"Eat it, Branco," Lukowsky shot back.

"One more uncalled for remark and you're out of here," Mr. Goodrich pointed a finger at Branco.

"Ooh, I'm terrified," Branco said in a high girlish voice that got the class tittering.

Mr. Goodrich walked over to the wall, picked up the phone, and called the office. "Please tell

Mr. Rope to expect a visit from Jeff Branco. I'm sending him down right now, and if he's not there in three minutes he'll be in even more trouble."

Mr. Goodrich held open the door. Jeff Branco got up slowly and sauntered across the room. As he passed Mr. Goodrich, he made a sudden move at him. Mr. Goodrich winced and scrunched up as if he was going to get hit, but Branco was just faking. He waved to us.

"Later, dudes." He went out.

Mr. Goodrich returned to his desk and sat down. He took some kind of inhaler out of the desk and breathed in with it. Then he patted his forehead with a handkerchief.

"Okay, where were we?" he asked.

"Sex scenes," Lukowsky said with a big grin.

Mr. Goodrich buried his head in his hands and groaned. Then the bell rang and everyone cleared out. When Mr. Goodrich looked up, I was the only one left in the room.

"Why haven't you loped out with the rest of the herd?" he asked.

"I think I made up my mind, Mr. G," I said. "I want to do the play."

"You do?" He looked surprised.

"Yeah."

Mr. Goodrich folded his handkerchief neatly and slid it back into his pocket. "This will require a serious commitment, Kyle. You'll have to learn your lines and come to rehearsals. The rest of the cast will be depending on you. If you can't take it more seriously than, uh . . ."

He trailed off like he didn't want to say what was coming next.

"More seriously than I take *school*, Mr. G?"

"I'm sorry, Kyle. I shouldn't have put it that way."

"It's okay," I said. "I'll give it my best shot."

"That's all I can ask for, Kyle." Mr. Goodrich stood up and offered his hand.

I shook it. It was sort of like shaking a dead fish.

BO

Today I told Mr. Goodrich I'd stage-manage *Anne Frank* after all. I changed my mind because I felt bad for him. Between Chloe and Kyle and all his other headaches, he doesn't need a stage manager who doesn't know what he or she is doing.

Of course, this is going to put a damper on my incredibly busy social life, but I'll just have to cope.

KYLE

Angie Sunberg's parties are kind of renowned because her parents have a big house and they usually make themselves scarce.

Chloe always likes to give the impression that she's got six social engagements a night, so even though Angie's party started at eight P.M. she told me not to pick her up until ten. I'll bet you anything she spent the time watching TV.

"Maybe we should do something else," I said after she got in the car.

Chloe gave me this look of disbelief. "Like what?"

"I don't know. Go to a movie or something."

"What about the party?"

I shrugged. "It's always the same thing. Same kids, same dumb stuff."

"But I thought you liked that."

"Guess I've changed."

"Everyone's expecting us."

So we went. We got to Angie's and it was the same old thing. A lot of people and noise and music and everyone acting crazy. Chloe was right. I used to love scenes like that. Now I almost dread them.

Chloe went off to chat with the girls and I hung out with my buds. Then Lukowsky must've said something crude to Angie because she slapped him pretty hard, and someone got the idea of tying Lukowsky up, so they raided the linen closet and got a bunch of sheets. They gagged him and wrapped him up like a mummy, then locked him in the downstairs powder room.

Later I was in the kitchen with Eddie and some of the guys. Pizza Hut had just delivered a Big Foot and we were chowing down. I have to admit that I was enjoying myself. I mean, if you can't play sports anymore, eating pizza and talking sports with the guys is probably the next best thing. I almost felt like I was on the team again.

Then Chloe came into the kitchen wearing her jacket and whispered in my ear, "I want to talk to you."

"What?" This caught me totally by surprise.

"Let's go outside."

"Why?"

Chloe obviously didn't want to say why in front of the guys. She just turned and left.

I grabbed my jacket and started to head out.

"Hey, bro," Eddie said.

"Yeah?" I stopped in the doorway.

"Married life's a drag, huh?" He winked.

I gave him the finger.

Outside Chloe was leaning on the car with her arms crossed. It was a clear, cool night and the stars were out. Cars lined both sides of the street—the universal sign of a party.

"I can't believe you didn't tell me you were going to be Peter," she said. "I had to find out from Beth Villeta. Do you know how embarrassing that is?"

"I was going to tell you," I said.

"When? At the first read-through?"

"No, I probably would have told you tonight."

Chloe glared at me. "Why?"

"Why what?"

"Why do you suddenly have to be in this play?"

"Why is it such a big deal?" I asked back.

Chloe let out a big sigh and stared up at the stars. "There are a million other things you could have done besides be in my play."

"*Your* play? Wow, Chloe, I didn't know you owned it."

Chloe gave me a withering look.

"I want to go home, Kyle."

Now I felt bad. Like maybe I should have

told her sooner. "Come on, Chloe. This is dumb." I stepped close and stroked her hair, but she turned away.

"I'm tired, Kyle. And my ankle hurts."

She didn't say a word on the way home. We got back to her house and she hopped out of the car and ran up the walk to the front door. It sure didn't look to me like her ankle was hurting.

BO

I was in such a good mood today. Rumor has it that Kyle and Chloe had a fight outside Angie Sunberg's house Saturday night. Then reality set in. Alice and Bobby were waiting for me on the catwalk.

"Ah, the welcoming committee," I said as I started to climb up the ladder.

"Look who decided to stage-manage *Anne Frank*," Bobby said.

"It's a free country," I said.

"Isn't she looking thinner?" Alice asked.

"I'm graduating this spring, and I don't want people to remember me as the understudy for the Goodyear blimp."

"Is that makeup you're wearing?" Bobby asked.

"Yes!" I cried. "I'm guilty. I've lost weight, put on makeup, and decided to be stage manager again. Bring on the gladiators! Throw me to the wolves!"

"This wouldn't have anything to do with a certain former football captain who's suddenly turned thespian, would it?" Bobby asked.

I stopped halfway up the ladder. He'd caught me completely off guard. "What? Of course not."

Bobby gave me that look. *He knew!* I couldn't believe it.

"There's no sense denying," Alice said.

I felt my shoulders sag. "It was the phone calls, right? Being so excited about talking to him, and asking about those football players who became actors. I knew I should have kept it to myself."

"That and the sudden change of mind concerning stage-managing," Bobby said. "Especially coming so soon after Kyle committed to doing Peter."

"So sue me."

"That's not the point," Alice said.

"Then what *is* the point?" I asked.

Alice and Bobby glanced at each other. I could see they'd prepared for this. They wanted to tell me THE TRUTH!

"Bo, we're talking about Kyle Winthrop," Bobby said.

"Please," I begged. "Don't do this to me. Don't foam the runway. Even if I'm flying blind, let me crash and burn on my own."

"It's for your own good," Alice said.

"I've heard that before. From every pediatrician who ever gave me a booster. From every orthodontist who ever tightened my braces."

"Stop being so dramatic." Alice sounded annoyed. "You only had one orthodontist and you know it."

"Excuse me for taking poetic license," I apologized.

"We don't want to see you get hurt," Bobby said.

"Thank you for that extreme vote of confidence," I said. "Thank you for thinking so highly of me."

"I hate it when you get maudlin," Alice said. "Be realistic."

"No," I said, and started to climb back down. "I won't be realistic and I won't take any more of this abuse. If I want to be insulted and ridiculed, I'll go home and let my mother do it."

"Wait," Bobby said. "You can stay. I have to go talk to Mr. G about the set budget anyway."

He started to climb down the other ladder. I headed back up toward Alice. I crossed the catwalk and sat down next to her. The air was stuffy and warmer than down below, but I didn't care.

"Did you hear what happened to Karl Lukowsky?" she asked.

"What now?"

"They tied him up at the party and left him

in the downstairs bathroom. Except Angie forgot he was there. They didn't find him till the next afternoon."

"Too bad," I said.

"That they forgot?"

"No, that they found him."

Alice pulled her knees up under her chin and gazed down at the stage below. I could see that she was depressed. Alice is a little awkward and she tends to wear baggy clothes and be quiet and unassuming. She looks a little depressed even when she's happy, so when she is depressed, she looks very depressed.

"Mr. G posted the cast list this morning," she said. "Why do these things always happen to me?"

"You can't be upset about being Mrs. Van Daan," I said. "Because you *knew* that's who you'd be."

"I know," said Alice. "Why do I always get the most unlikable parts?"

"Because you're the best actress in school," I said.

"If I'm the best actress, why does Chloe get the leads?" asked Alice.

"Because she's a star," I said.

"Just for once I'd like to be a star," Alice said wistfully.

Wouldn't we all.

KYLE

Tonight I was listening to this tape Eddie lent me. It's by this singer named Meatloaf. The whole tape is pretty good, but it has one totally outstanding number called "Paradise by the Dashboard Light." Knowing me and Chloe, Eddie thought I'd appreciate it. He was right.

So I was in my room listening to it, and all of a sudden I looked up and there was Jackie standing in my doorway with this goofy smile on her face and IT drooling in her arms.

"I love that song," she said.

I looked at her for a moment, and then looked away. What was I supposed to say? Meanwhile, Jackie stood there waiting for me to say something. Out of the corner of my eye I saw the smile slowly evaporate from her face, sort of like someone who thinks a joke is being played on them. Finally she just turned and left.

I guess she was upset. Maybe she thought that because we both liked that song it finally gave us something in common. Us and about fifteen million other people.

BO

At the end of a play the actors take their bows. Sometimes they'll bring out the director to take a bow and then gesture to the orchestra conductor and the musicians and they'll all take bows. Occasionally, if the playwright is present, he or she will even take a bow.

You will never see the stage manager take a bow. I toil in anonymity at a difficult, thankless task in which I act as a marriage counselor, divorce lawyer, mother, and foreman to the rest of the cast and crew. It is my role to coordinate the entire production, to make sure all the pieces of the puzzle—cast, crew, sets, props, and costumes—fit together. It is my job to nag and badger and soothe and commiserate. I will be blamed for everything that goes wrong and never appreciated for all the things that go right. And in the end, when the curtain falls for the last time, I won't be out there basking in the warm glow of applause like the rest of them.

Worst of all, I will have to deal with Karl "The Letch" Lukowsky, who runs AV.

Step inside the AV room and you enter a time warp. Where else do you find guys (it's very rare to find a female AV person) who still wear bell bottoms and have shaggy haircuts? Where else do they still listen to the Grateful Dead and Led Zeppelin? Where else do they still read *Mad Magazine*?

But from somewhere in the dank dark depths of that room will come the "techie" I'll depend on to handle the lights, curtain, and sound cues for the show. If I'm lucky, he won't skin his knuckles when he walks.

"Hey, lookin' good, babe." Inside the AV room The Letch leered at me through the industrial shelving holding film projectors and VCRs. The Letch has a shaggy haircut, buck teeth, and a case of acne that makes his face resemble a relief map of the Alps. Subscribing to the (misguided) theory that he who has the most keys is the most important, he wears a key ring with enough keys to open the doors of a small city.

"I hear you've been spending a lot of time in bathrooms lately," I said.

The Letch just laughed. "Har, har, har."

"I need a techie for the play."

"No problemo, babe." The Letch must be

twenty years old. I think he keeps getting left back because the only place he feels at home in is the AV room. Or because there's no such thing as janitor's college.

"We're going to need lights, curtains, and some sound cues."

"No problemo, babe."

"It would be nice if you pick someone who can be available for all the run-throughs and dress rehearsals."

"No problemo, babe."

"I'd appreciate it if you stopped calling me babe."

"Har, har, no problemo . . . er, honey."

KYLE

In the boys' room today, instead of the usual cigarette smoke and bathroom odors, it smelled like pizza. I was in there minding my own business when two freshmen came in and went down to the third toilet stall and knocked.

"Yeah?" answered someone inside the stall.

"Joey sent us," one of the kids said.

"How many?" asked the person inside the stall.

"Two."

"Okay. Four bucks."

The next thing I knew, one of the freshmen kneeled down and slid four bills under the door. A second later two slices of pizza on paper plates came sliding out. The freshmen took them and left.

I went down to the stall and knocked.

"Yeah?" the voice answered.

"Arnie sent me."

"Arnie? I don't know no Arnie."

"How about Ralph?" I asked.

"Get lost."

"Hey, Jeff, it's me, Kyle."

The stall door opened. Inside, Jeff Branco had four pizza boxes stacked on the toilet seat. "Yo, Kyle," he said, slapping me five.

"When did you get into the pizza business?" I asked.

"I got a friend who delivers for Sal's Pizza in town," Jeff said, handing me a slice. "Whenever Sal ain't around, my friend cops a few pies, brings 'em over here and slides 'em through the bathroom window to me. We split the profits. Tell me this ain't superior to that junk the cafeteria sells."

A couple of sophomores came in and bought four slices. Jeff pocketed the money.

"I never knew you were such an entrepreneur," I said, only half-kidding. I always thought he was just a hood. Who could have guessed he had the brains to think up something like this?

"I gotta score some heavy dollars," Jeff said. "Special occasion coming up."

I finished the slice he gave me. "Well, thanks."

"Sure," Jeff said. "Hey, Kyle, you want in?"

"Huh?"

"I'm thinking of franchising. They got six boys' rooms in the school. That's six pizza franchises. I'll even cut you a deal 'cause you're one of us."

One of them?

"Uh, thanks for the offer, Jeff. Let me think about it."

I got out in the hall and started walking. *One of them? Me?* I never thought I was one of them.

BO

This afternoon I ventured to The Gap and invested in a new wardrobe. Nothing fancy, just some jeans and tops. But the tops were mediums and the jeans were size ten. It's amazing how much difference eight pounds can make. Then I went home and packed some of my old clothes in a box and left it by the front door.

A little while ago my mother came in.

"What are those things doing in that box by the front door?" she asked.

"The Salvation Army is going to pick them up tomorrow," I said.

"Those are perfectly good clothes," she said.

"Except they're too big," I said.

"I am not going to buy you a whole new wardrobe when you gain the weight back," she said.

"Thanks for the encouragement," I grumbled.

My mother blinked at the shock of realization. "You're right. I'm sorry."

"I'm losing weight gradually. I really think it's going to work."

My mother stared at me. "What's gotten into you?"

Not that I'd ever tell her.

KYLE

Here are the first ten lines Peter speaks in the play:

1. "Please, Mother."
2. "Yes, Mrs. Frank."
3. "Mouschi." (the cat)
4. "He's a tom. He doesn't like strangers."
5. "Huh?"
6. "No."
7. "Jewish Secondary."
8. "I used to see you . . . sometimes."
9. "In the schoolyard. You were always in the middle of a bunch of kids."
10. "I'm sort of a lone wolf."

More like a lone wimp. Do I really want to be this guy?

BO

Tonight after swimming I was coming out of the girls' locker room when someone came in through the pool doors. I didn't really get a good look at the person because I was busy pulling my fingers through my wet stringy hair, having forgotten to bring a brush. Suddenly the person stopped in my path, and I looked up. It was Kyle.

"Oh, it's you!" I said.

"How come you're always so surprised to see me?" he asked.

I waited for that nervous inadequate sensation to take hold and wrap me in its straitjacket of fear. But for some reason it didn't.

"I'm not sure it's so much surprise as embarrassment," I said, grabbing the wet ends of my hair in my fists and tugging at them. "I mean, look at me."

"You look like you have wet hair," Kyle said. "I think it would be really tough to swim and then have dry hair."

"Some people bring a hair dryer," I said.

"That doesn't seem like something you'd do."

I guess I gave him a startled look. "How would you know that?"

Kyle smiled rather sheepishly. "I don't know. Just a feeling, I guess."

Suddenly I remembered something. I opened my bag and took out a playbook. "This is for you."

"Thanks, but Mr. G already gave me a copy," Kyle said.

"Not like this."

Kyle opened the book and thumbed through it. Then he looked up at me with surprise on his face. "You highlighted my lines."

"You really don't have to learn the other parts," I said, "as long as you know when you're supposed to speak."

"That's really nice of you."

"One of my jobs is to make it easier for the greenhorns," I explained. Although, the truth was, I'd never done anything like that before.

Kyle slipped the playbook into his jacket pocket. "Maybe I should talk to you about that."

"About what?"

"This play. It's uh . . ." Kyle glanced past me at the pool and changed the topic. "What's the water like tonight?"

"Just slightly warmer than glacial," I said.

He winced. I could see he wasn't keen about throwing himself into the chilly, chlorinated depths. Then I did the most outrageous thing. I mean, I still can't believe I said, "Want to go to the diner?"

(Before I go any further, let me state clearly that I have never in my life tried to steal another girl's boyfriend. Moreover, had I honestly believed that there was even the remotest possibility that Kyle had a romantic interest in me, I would never have suggested going to the diner. I would have suggested a much more romantic setting, such as the dock at the Post Point Yacht Club.)

Meanwhile Kyle only scowled. I suddenly froze in terror over what I'd done. Look out! Foam the runway! Crash landing! He's going to say no. He's going to reject me. He's going to tell all his friends. I'll be the laughing stock of the entire school! Oh, why didn't I listen to Bobby and Alice? Kyle started to open his mouth, but there was still time to avert disaster.

"On second thought, it was dumb of me to suggest that," I quickly said. "I mean, you came here to swim. The last thing you probably want to do is eat. I really don't know why I suggested it. Let's just forget it."

"You're right," he said. "It's bad enough that I'm not gonna swim, but going to the diner's only gonna make it worse."

Hold it! Had I heard him correctly? Did he say he *wasn't* going swimming? Maybe I'd misunderstood. But Kyle turned and held the door for me. The next thing I knew, we were walking out in the cold air toward the darkened cars in the parking lot.

"So where do you want to go?" he asked.

"Uh, I don't know." I was still in shock.

"Well, want to take one car or two?"

"Unless you're into grand felony auto theft, we better take one."

Kyle gave me a funny look, then smiled. "I get it. You didn't drive here."

"Not here, not anywhere."

"Don't you have your license?" he asked.

"I believe the world is a safer place without me behind the wheel," I said.

Being all but oblivious to the universe of automobiles, I can only tell you that Kyle's car was small and possibly of Asian origin. We wound up at the Post Point Yacht Club. Believe me, I wouldn't have suggested it, except that Kyle clearly didn't want to do anything that involved increasing his daily caloric intake.

"Isn't this trespassing?" he asked as we climbed over a low metal gate and walked around the dark porch of the club.

"Only if we get caught."

We walked out to the end of the dock. It was

cold and breezy. Small waves were splashing against the pilings. The moon was three-quarters full and a pair of sea gulls hovered almost perfectly still in the night sky, riding the wind.

"Come here a lot?" Kyle asked.

"No."

"No?"

"Just on nights when the moon is almost full and it's a little too cold and I'm with someone who doesn't want to eat," I said. I could feel the cold breeze sting my face and a single thought floated in my mind: *What in the world am I doing here with him?*

Kyle turned and looked down the shoreline.

"What are you looking at?" I asked.

"Chloe's house."

"Where?" I knew Chloe's father was a doctor and they were well-off, but I'd always thought the people who could afford homes on the water were in the socio-economic stratosphere.

"Over there." Kyle pointed. It was hard to see in the dark. Several very large houses stood beside the harbor, windows lit, their tall, dim silhouettes just visible against the night sky, their lawns sloping down to stone sea walls and private docks. I couldn't tell exactly which house Kyle meant. Maybe it didn't matter.

"What's she doing tonight?" I asked.

"Got me."

What did *that* mean? Did he wish he was with her and not me? Were they having problems? Maybe they didn't like each other anymore. Kyle turned back to me and slid his hands into the pockets of his pants. "I'm kind of glad I ran into you."

"Because I saved you from swimming?"

"No, it's about the play."

"That's right. You said something was bothering you."

"Peter's sort of a geek," Kyle said. "His father's a jerk. And in a way, it's Peter's fault that Anne and everybody gets caught and sent to concentration camps."

"It's only a role," I said. "It's not something that reflects on you personally."

"I just wish he wasn't such a wimp," Kyle said.

"I promise no one is going to think of you as a wimp-by-association."

Kyle smiled a little and muttered something about going from athletic to pathetic.

"What?" I asked.

"Nothing."

The dock rocked slightly as the waves rolled under it. It was a little like trying to stand up in a boat. I looked up and noticed the sea gulls had vanished. Kyle was glancing at his watch. I was starting to shiver.

"We can go," I said, not wanting him to feel

like he was stuck with me.

"I could probably catch the last quarter of Tulane and SMU," he said.

He drove me home. Did it mean that given the choice between watching football and being with me, Kyle would choose football?

Don't answer that.

KYLE

There's this girl at school whose name (you won't believe this) is Bo Vine. Bo is short for something, but it doesn't matter because everyone calls her Bovine. Like a cow. To make it worse, she's always been on the chunky side. I remember in grade school and junior high she really got kidded a lot, like to the point of tears a couple of times.

When Jake was about a year old, Bovine started to baby-sit for him every once in a while. I saw her at the house a couple of times, but I never said more than hello because I didn't know her or anything. Well, that's not the total truth. I didn't talk to her much because she seemed kind of strange. Maybe it was because she got picked on so much when she was younger. Or maybe because now she just sort of keeps to herself at school and never talks to anyone except a couple of her friends in the theater group.

The other thing is, except for her classes, she spends almost all her time on this catwalk above the stage. Like she's a pigeon or something.

Anyway, now I see her almost every day because she's the stage manager for the play. I've seen her at the pool a couple of times, too. It actually looks like she's lost some weight, which is more than I can say for myself.

So tonight we ran into each other at the pool and wound up at this yacht club standing on the dock. She's got a kind of quiet, sarcastic sense of humor, and I sort of enjoyed talking to her.

Especially since Chloe and I don't have much to say to each other these days.

BO

On Saturday afternoon Alice wasn't around so I begged Bobby to drive me to the mall.

"There's a bus, you know," he said.

"I need moral support."

"You need moral support to go to the mall?" He raised a blond eyebrow. "That's a new one."

"You'll see," I said.

When we got there, I dragged him to Hair Affair, a unisex salon. Inside, three hair stylists instantly crowded around him, just dying to get their hands on his long, beautiful blond dreadlocks.

"Sorry, girls, I'm not the one," he said, and pointed at me.

You never saw such looks of disappointment.

An hour and a half later my hair was done.

And I mean *done*.

Where it used to be straight, dull, and brown, it was now a glorious shade of auburn and flowed onto my shoulders in waves.

"You look great! We have to celebrate!" Bobby led me by the hand to The Slice of Life pizzeria. Inside we sat on bent wire chairs around a little red plastic table. The walls were lined with mirrors and that's where I saw myself, not in the make-believe world of Hair Affair, but in the real world of discarded pizza crusts, twelve-year-olds smoking cigarettes, and young women with too much eye makeup, red stiletto nails, and big hair.

The effect was devastating. I suddenly realized I was doomed.

"Why the long face?" Bobby asked as he sprinkled garlic and oregano on his pizza.

"You'd have a long face, too, if you'd just signed your own death warrant."

Bobby scowled. "What are you talking about?"

"Do you have any idea what I'm going to face in school on Monday morning? I can just hear them. 'Did you see Bovine?' 'Who does she think she is?' 'Maybe she can change what's on the outside, but she'll never change what's on the inside.'"

Bobby scowled at me. "What's wrong with your insides?"

I was plummeting so fast into new hair despair that I hardly heard him. "Why did I do this?" I moaned. "Who am I kidding? Why did I have to be so stupidly obvious? Did I really think I could go from Jabba the Hut to Princess Leia overnight?"

"Bo . . ." Bobby looked alarmed.

"That's right, I'm Bo. Bovine. The cow. Did you ever see that Amazon movie where they throw the cow in the river and the piranhas get it? Three minutes later all that's left is a skeleton. That's going to be me Monday morning. It's going to be a feeding frenzy . . . a massacre."

I was seized by a dread so great I began to hyperventilate. The thought of walking into school on Monday filled me with a terror a hundred times worse than a visit to The Dentist From Hell. I was a sitting duck, a sacrificial lamb, a big round jack-o'-lantern on Halloween night. . . .

I jumped up.

"Where are you going?" Bobby asked.

"Back to Hair Affair!" I gasped. "I have to get rid of this hair. I have to get back to mousy old unattractive me before someone notices!"

"Stop!" Bobby shouted.

I froze, suddenly aware that everyone in The Slice of Life was staring at me. The swarthy countermen with dark stubble on their chins and tomato sauce stains on their white T-shirts, the twelve-year-olds smoking their first Marlboros, the big-hair girls with their raccoon eyelids and garden-stake fingernails, the overweight grandmothers with their shopping bags—every single one of them was staring.

Bobby stood up and pointed at me.

"Will you look at her hair?" he said to everyone.

"Please don't, Bobby . . ." I whimpered. My face was burning. I was dying of embarrassment.

"Doesn't she look great?" Bobby asked.

Around The Slice of Life heads bobbed.

"Bobby, please . . ." I begged.

"Would you believe she's terrified that the kids at school are going to laugh at her?" Bobby asked.

"No way. She looks gorgeous," said one of the countermen.

"What do you care what other people think?" asked one of the big-hair girls.

"They're just jealous, honey," said one of the overweight grandmothers.

"Uh, thanks, everyone," I said to them all. "You see I just got it done and it's really a big change for me and, well, you know . . ."

"If anyone laughs at you, smash 'em in the face," said one of the twelve-year-old Marlboro smokers.

Bobby gave me a triumphant smile. "See? You have nothing to worry about."

"Can we get out of here?" I whispered.

Bobby grabbed his slice. We waved at my

impromptu support group and left.

"Smash 'em in the face!" Bobby and I were laughing so hard we practically tumbled down the handicapped ramp as we staggered past Foot Locker and Bed Bath & Beyond. I gave him a gentle shove. "I can't believe you did that!"

"What makes you think you're so unique?" Bobby asked. "I mean, aren't you being a little egocentric?"

"Of course," I said. "But you still can't deny that people are going to talk when they notice something different Monday morning."

"And you think you're the only one who looks different? You don't think that people notice I have shoulder-length blond dreadlocks?"

"But they're used to you," I said. "And besides, you're gorgeous."

"Do you think it's easy to be a gorgeous boy?" Bobby asked. "I mean, God, Bo, all you have to do is go to school on Monday looking pretty."

I'd never thought of it that way.

KYLE

About ten minutes ago, Jackie called my father into the nursery.

"He's got diarrhea," I heard her say.

"Remember what the doctor said," my father replied calmly. "It's not the consistency, it's how often they go. It's not diarrhea unless he goes four or more times in one day."

My father, the diarrhea expert.

"I'm just worried," Jackie said.

"Didn't the doctor say it was common in babies while they're teething?" my father asked.

"What if this is something else?" Jackie asked.

"Let's wait a day and see what happens."

While they're having this conversation, guess who waddled into the den with pink drool dripping off his chin?

"Wha dat?" he pointed at the magazine I was reading.

"A movie," I said.

"Mooey, mooey," he said, and waddled off toward the nursery.

BO

I asked Alice to meet me in the parking lot before school started. I stood between some cars. It was a cold, gray day. The last few yellowed leaves were falling from the trees.

A voice cried out from behind me, "Bo, is that you?"

I turned. Alice stood there with her mouth agape.

"What do you think?" I asked.

"Halloween was three weeks ago," she said. But then she smiled. "Just kidding."

"It's not funny!"

"No, I like it, really," Alice said. "It's just so different. I mean, if you did this as a before and after in *Vogue* no one would believe it was the same person."

❖　❖　❖

In terms of my emergence in a new form, the inhabitants of Time Zone High can be divided into four groups:

1. Those who didn't notice. (Most)

2. Those who noticed and thought it was someone new. (Some)

3. Those who noticed and realized it was me but didn't say anything. (Several)

4. Those who noticed and realized it was me and said something. (A few)

The Few Who Spoke:

Mr. Goodrich: (Eyes wide, startled expression) "Bo! Is that you?"

Bobby: "Now, is this so bad?"

The Letch: "Woof!"

At lunch I waited until after the bell and then went into the girls' room to check my makeup. I thought I had the bathroom to myself, but then the door swung open and Chloe dashed in, as if she was trying to avoid someone. I watched her catch her breath. Then she went straight to the mirror and started primping.

I froze. She glanced at me, then back at herself, then did a double take.

"Bo?" she said.

"Oh, hi, Chloe." I'm so subtle.

"You . . . you look . . ."

I'm not sure I'd ever seen Chloe tongue-tied before. I braced myself for some clever, cutting remark.

Finally, Chloe got it out. "You look great."

I wanted to kill her.

KYLE

Some people have built-in radar. Take Chloe. Usually I'll pass her a couple of times a day in the hall and see her at least once in the senior lounge. But I haven't seen her since the party. That's what I mean by radar. She must sense me in the hall and hide long before I have a chance to notice her.

I usually don't go over to her house during the week because she's too busy studying, but tonight I did. Mrs. Frost peeked through the little window in the door and saw me outside. I caught a glimpse of the surprised look on her face, but then she made a superfast recovery and smiled warmly.

"Kyle, what a surprise," she said, pulling the door open. "Come in. I'll get Chloe."

Chloe's mom disappeared down the hall. She's always been kind of warm, but distant with me. I get the feeling she thinks of me as a "phase" in Chloe's life. Like someday she'll get out the family album and show some visitor Chloe's baby pictures. And then maybe a picture of Chloe with her Barbie dolls during her "Barbie phase" and a photo of Chloe on her horse during her "horse phase" and then a photo of Chloe with me during her "Kyle phase."

I stood in the entryway and waited. Near the door was a security keypad with half a dozen tiny red and green lights. Chloe once told me they even had sensors under the lawn so that if someone stepped on it at night the alarm would go off. I guess you can never be too safe.

After about ten minutes—which meant Chloe was putting on her makeup and fixing her hair—she came to the top of the stairs, dressed like she was ready to go out. Except it was ten thirty on a weekday night and she wasn't going anywhere.

"Surprise, surprise," she said.

"I was in the neighborhood and thought I'd stop by. Haven't seen you around school much."

"I've been hard to find," Chloe said.

I wasn't sure what she meant by that. "I thought maybe we should talk."

Chloe didn't look thrilled, but she said, "Come up."

Chloe's bedroom is like an office. She's got a bed and dressers and posters on the walls like everyone else, but the thing you notice most is this big black lacquer desk with a PowerBook and a printer, an ink blotter, a telephone, and a fax machine. On the wall beside the desk are shelves filled with books and paper and supplies.

Chloe sat down at the desk. "Why didn't you just call?"

"Because I wanted to talk."

Chloe frowned a little.

"Sometimes when we talk on the phone," I said, "I feel like you're doing three other things at the same time."

Chloe didn't deny it. She looked down at some papers on her desk, then back at me. "What did you want to talk about?"

"Us."

Her eyes narrowed slightly.

"Look," I said, "maybe I should try to explain to you why I decided to—"

"Because you were a star, Kyle." Chloe decided to explain for me. "You were a hero. You were the captain of the football team and basked in everyone's adoration. Even teachers were afraid to offend you. It must be terrible not to have that anymore, so you're trying to find it somewhere else."

I guess deep down I knew there was some truth to that. "You're not jealous, are you?"

Chloe has this way of reacting by not

reacting. It's almost like, the bigger the impact of the question, the less she shows it.

"It's more like a feeling of being violated."

"Huh?"

Chloe looked back at the papers and toyed with a loose paper clip for a moment.

"You mean, it's like I don't belong in the play?"

"Do you?"

"Look, I'm not going to make acting a career," I said. "It's just something I feel like trying."

"All the world's a stage, and all the men and women merely players," she said as if reciting a poem.

"What's that?"

"Shakespeare."

"You really wish I wasn't in the play?" I asked.

"It doesn't matter."

"It doesn't matter because I'm already in it, or it doesn't matter because you don't care?"

"It's too hard to explain."

I got up and pulled on my jacket. I guess I'd had enough of her mysterious attitude for one night. "Maybe it is too hard to explain," I said. "Or maybe, for once, you just don't have an answer."

BO

Bobby and I were sitting on the catwalk at lunch today. The school band was practicing on the stage below us.

"God, they're awful," Bobby whispered.

"They're not awful," I replied. "They're high school."

"Why does everything in high school have to be so unprofessional?" Bobby asked. "Can't we raise our standards?"

I stared at him. "You're starting to sound like Chloe."

Bobby locked his eyes on mine. "Have you noticed that we can't have a conversation without you bringing up Chloe? No matter what we talk about, it always winds up being about her."

"Not true," I said.

"It is, Bo. You're obsessed."

I didn't answer. But inside I suspected he was right. Only I wasn't sure if it was Chloe I was obsessed with . . . or her boyfriend.

KYLE

We read through the play today. Mr. Goodrich said we were just supposed to read our lines, not act, but you should have seen Chloe. At the point where Mrs. Frank wants to kick the Van Daans out because Mr. Van Daan was stealing bread, I really thought Chloe was going to throw herself on the stage floor. I won't be surprised if she does it during the performance.

After the read-through, Mr. Goodrich told everyone to go home. Chloe and I had sort of made up after what happened the other night, but she still took off like a shot. She's driving again so she doesn't need me to chauffeur her around.

I waited until I thought everyone had left. But when I went back out to the stage, Mr. Goodrich was there talking to Bo. I almost didn't recognize her. Looks like she changed her hair and decided to really bone up on her makeup skills. Anyway, both she and Mr. Goodrich looked surprised to see me.

"Seems like I'm always interrupting you two," I said.

"That's okay, Kyle," Mr. Goodrich said. "What's up?"

I didn't want to talk in front of Bo. She got the hint pretty quick and went backstage.

"Is something wrong, Kyle?" Mr. Goodrich asked.

"I hate to say this, Mr. G," I said, "but I'm having doubts about the play."

Mr. Goodrich nodded. "Right now it must look overwhelming. The lines, the stage directions, working with actors and actresses you don't know. That's why we'll rehearse for so long. By the time we open, a month and a half from now, you'll know your lines, blocking, and the other actors better than you know your own family."

He patted me on the shoulder. "The only difference between you and the rest of the cast is that they've all been through this before. Believe me, there have been plenty of times when they wanted to quit, too."

I believed him, but I wasn't sure it made it any better.

"Is there something else, Kyle?" Mr. Goodrich asked.

There was. It was something that had been

bothering me ever since I read the play, but until that moment I'd never been able to put it into words.

"It's a true story, isn't it? I mean, what happened to the Franks and Van Daans."

Mr. Goodrich looked a little surprised. "Why yes, of course."

"I don't get it. They were just ordinary people. They weren't in the army. They had nothing to do with the war. They didn't do anything wrong."

"That's the tragedy of the story," Mr. Goodrich said. "Anne was a sweet impetuous young girl. Stifled and confined at a time of her life when she should have been growing and free."

"Then she dies for no reason," I said.

"Millions died for no reason," Mr. Goodrich said. "Children, mothers . . . The greatest horror of modern history. That's what makes this such a powerful play, Kyle. Anne Frank was an everyday person like you and me, and yet this is what happened to her."

"Isn't there another play we could do?" I asked.

Mr. Goodrich seemed sort of surprised. "Well, yes, I suppose, but few have the kind of impact this play has. It's such an important lesson about good and evil and hope. Think of the service you'll be doing by performing it."

"Well, that's just it," I said.

"What's just it?" Mr. Goodrich looked puzzled.

"I guess the thing that really gets me is that this is such a serious play," I said. "I've never acted in a play before and I'd feel really bad if I blew this."

"I assure you, Kyle, you won't," said Mr. Goodrich.

It was nice of him to say that, but let's get real, folks. How does he know?

BO

I followed Kyle into the parking lot. It was dark and cold and the moon was going in and out of the clouds. "Wait!"

He turned around. I could barely make out the features of his face in the shadows. He looked surprised. "Oh, hi."

"This time you're the one who looks surprised," I said. My heart was beating fast. I didn't know whether it was from running, or just being near him again. "I heard what you said to Mr. G."

"You listened?"

I nodded. "Do you hate me?"

Kyle bent his head and ran his fingers through his hair. "I guess it doesn't matter."

"I just wanted to tell you not to worry so much about making a mistake," I said. "That's what rehearsals are for."

"Even after a hundred rehearsals you can still go out and drop the ball."

"Everyone flubs a line now and then," I said. "A good actor just keeps right on going and carries the audience with him."

"And a bad actor?"

"Does the same thing, just not as well."

Kyle smiled slightly in the dark.

"Guess I'm on a new team," he said. "Only instead of being a linebacker, I'll probably be a line-hacker. Anyway, need a ride?"

"Uh, okay."

We got in his car. I fought the temptation to ask why Chloe had left so quickly before. Instead, I just basked in the thought that he was driving me home and not her.

"I noticed you changed your hair," he said as we pulled out of the parking lot.

"You like it?" I asked.

Kyle glanced over at me. I smiled back. Perhaps this is one of the great differences between the sexes. Females notice something looks different and decide right away whether they like it or not. Males simply notice that something is different. Deciding whether they like it is a whole separate thought process.

"Yeah, I do."

I'm in love! I thought.

KYLE

I was heading for the football table with my lunch tray.

"Yo, Kyle!" Lukowsky waved at me from the Pinhead table where he was sitting with Branco, the Rat, and the others.

"What's up?" I asked.

"Heard you're in the play."

"Yeah."

Suddenly they all pulled out pens and pieces of paper. "Can we have your autograph?"

"You guys are such jerks," I said with a smile.

"No, man, we want to say we knew you when," said the Rat.

This cracked the rest of the Pinheads up. One thing you can say for these guys, they may be misfits, but they have a sense of humor.

The laughter died down and an awkward moment followed. Like I could go to class with them, I could joke with them, but somehow, I wasn't one of them.

"Later, guys," I said, and headed over to the football table.

"Hey, bro, what's this about you bein' in a play?" Eddie asked as I sat down. "How come you didn't tell us?"

"I don't know. Guess I wasn't sure I was gonna stay with it."

"So is this your new career?" Alex Gidden asked.

"Nah, it's just something to do."

"Chloe must've talked him into it," Jason said sort of snidely.

"Actually, she's really against it."

The guys gave me these looks like they were amazed to hear this. It's like everyone assumes Chloe directs my life. Like I need her permission to do things. Maybe they thought I was her robot or something.

"Isn't she in the play, too?" Eddie asked.

"Yeah."

The guys scowled at each other. Like this didn't make *any* sense to them at all.

BO

This morning I left a note in the AV room for The Letch to send my techie to the auditorium during lunch.

Later I was sitting on the stage with Bobby trying to estimate how much paint we'd need when The Letch himself strolled down the aisle.

"Here I am, babe," he said.

Bobby and I glanced at each other. "You're the techie?" I asked.

"Yup."

"Don't you usually send one of your gremlins to do it?"

"No one's available," said The Letch. I could feel him undressing me with his eyes. No one had ever done that before. . . . I might've enjoyed it if it wasn't The Letch.

"So when do we start?" he asked.

"I'll let you know," I said, turning back to Bobby.

The Letch wouldn't know a hint if Jimi Hendrix walked in and played it for him. Instead of leaving, he said he wanted to check the lights. He climbed up on stage and proceeded to test every light in the house. It was so distracting that Bobby and I finally went to the lunch room.

I'm not a mean person. Believe me, I can't afford to be. But if The Letch were the last man on Earth, I would become a lesbian.

KYLE

Nobody ever asked if I wanted to be a Pinhead. The decision was made for me. After my mother died, I began to get into trouble. They started calling my father in for conferences. Then I was sent to the school shrink who gave me a bunch of tests. And the next thing I knew, I was in the PINS.

I think deep down most of the Pinheads would rather be with the "normal" kids, but they cover it up by acting goofy and pretending they don't care. I never really cared, mostly because I had football.

I'm the only athlete in the PINS. The Rat was on the cross-country team for a while, but they could never get him to run in the right direction.

Anyway, I was hanging out in the senior lounge after school today, waiting for rehearsal to start, when Mr. Orillio walked by.

"Hey, Mr. O." I gave him a wave.

"Hey, Kyle." He waved back. Then he must have thought of something because he stopped. "Say, you got a minute?"

I glanced across the hall at the auditorium. Ben McGillis and Beth Villeta were already on the stage, but most of the others hadn't arrived yet.

"Uh, sure. What's up?"

"Come out to my car with me," he said.

I gave him a questioning look.

"Hey, only my wife gets to look at me that way." He winked.

We went out to this old beat-up yellow Volvo, and he opened the trunk. Inside, was the typical trunk stuff like a spare tire and some rags and jugs of windshield washer fluid. There was also a ragged cardboard box filled with old record albums.

"Let's see now." Mr. Orillio thumbed through the albums. He pulled one out and handed it to me. On the cover were five guys with long hair, white bell-bottoms, and granny glasses. The group was called The Bongs and the album featured the hit single "Gettin' By on Love."

"This is from the sixties, right?" I asked.

"Very good, Kyle. It was made in 1968." Mr. Orillio got into the car and motioned me to join him.

"We going somewhere?" I asked as I got in.

"Back in time," Mr. Orillio said as he slid a tape into his dashboard cassette player. This tinny rock music started to play. Mr. Orillio turned the volume up.

When you see me comin' down the street
I look like someone you would like to meet.
I got this feelin' fits me like a glove
Cause baby, I'm gettin' by on love . . .

"I've heard that," I said.

"Oh, yeah, they still play it on the oldies stations," Mr. Orillio said. "We were number one for three weeks that summer."

"What do you mean, *we*?"

"Take a look." He tapped the album cover.

I looked closer at the cover and noticed that one of The Bongs was short and had frizzed-out hair like Jimi Hendrix. His shirt sleeves were rolled up and his arms were crossed. They were hairy arms.

I looked back at Mr. Orillio and felt my jaw drop. "No way . . ."

"Yes, way," Mr. Orillio said. "We opened for The Strawberry Alarm Clock, Traffic, The Kinks, Big Brother, The Jefferson Airplane, The Blues Project, Paul Butterfield, The Yardbirds . . ."

"Who?" I asked.

"You've never heard of the Yardbirds?"

"I've never heard of any of them."

Mr. Orillio looked disappointed. "I must be getting old. They were big groups, Kyle. The only ones bigger were the Beatles, the Stones, and Led Zep."

"That's incredible, Mr. O. What did you play?"

"Rhythm guitar," Mr. Orillio said. "We were on TV, Kyle. *American Bandstand, The Smothers Brothers Show*. We played the west coast, Europe—"

"Woodstock?"

Mr. Orillio shook his head. "We were done by then."

"Done?"

"Our second album bombed. The record company dropped us like a hot potato. We went from playing five-thousand-seat halls in San Francisco and New York to two-hundred-seat clubs in Toledo, Ohio. After five months of that the band broke up."

"Bummer, Mr. O."

"You're telling me," he said. "One week we were met at the airport by a limo. The next week we were driving around in a beat-up van with our amps tied to the roof."

"So what'd you do?"

"Went back to college and got a teaching degree." Mr. Orillio hit the eject button and the tape popped out.

"Anyone at school know about this?" I asked.

"A few."

"How come you told me?"

Mr. Orillio just gazed at me for a moment. "Because I wanted to show you that life goes on, Kyle. You don't give up just because they turn off the spotlight."

I stared down at the frizzy-haired musician on the cover of the album. "You weren't a Pinhead."

"No, I wasn't, Kyle. And I wasn't a big good-looking guy like you either. We all get dealt a hand. Whether we like it or not, those are the cards we have to play with."

I knew what he was saying was probably true, but I also felt like I'd heard enough. Maybe there's a limit to how much wisdom you can absorb at any given time.

"Yeah, thanks," I said. "Gotta get back to rehearsal." I started to get out of the car, but Mr. Orillio grabbed my arm.

"Just one last thing, Kyle."

"What?"

"It's better to be a has-been than a never-was."

"Huh?"

"Think about it."

BO

Today at lunch Alice drove me to the county clerk's office. Alice is terrified of driving and travels everywhere at speeds five to ten miles an hour under the legal limit. She leans forward so that her face is only inches from the windshield and grips the wheel so tightly that her knuckles turn white. She's about the most unrelaxed driver I've ever seen.

"Would you please stop humming?" she snapped.

"Huh? I didn't realize I was," I said.

"You've been humming for days. I've never seen you in such a good mood. It's scary."

"Sorry."

"Did something happen with Kyle?"

"No." Nothing that I'd want to talk about, anyway.

"You know, Mr. G isn't very happy about him," Alice said.

"He'll loosen up."

"Bo, if he were any more wooden he'd be a cigar-store Indian."

◇　◇　◇

Alice stayed in the car while I went into town hall. About half an hour later I returned.

"You took so long!" Alice gasped, pointing at the digital clock in her dashboard. "We're going to be late."

"It was worth it," I said.

"What did you find out?" She inched her car out of the parking lot.

"It was very intelligent of me not to get a driver's license, credit cards, or open any bank accounts," I said.

"Why?" asked Alice, since we were both aware that at least two of those items were things most people our age can't wait to get.

"Because it will make it easier for me to change my name," I said.

KYLE

I was sitting in the den watching monster trucks crush piles of junked cars. I don't know what it has to do with sports, but it's fun to watch. It was dinner time, and I was eating a giant peanut butter and jelly sandwich on French bread. The front door opened and my father came in. His collar was pulled open and his tie was loose. Looked like he'd had a bad day.

"Where's Jackie?" he asked, pulling off his coat.

"Don't know."

"Anything for dinner?"

"Choose-your-own-adventure."

"Great," he grumbled.

The front door opened again and Jackie came in carrying a sleeping IT swaddled in a light blue blanket.

"Where were you?" my father asked.

"I took Jake to see Dr. Huber."

"Again? That's the third time this month. What's wrong now?"

"He wasn't acting right." Jackie started down the hall toward the nursery.

"Wasn't acting right?" my father called after her. "What does that mean?"

"Would you keep your voice down? You'll wake him."

My father turned to me. "He wasn't acting right so she took him to the doctor."

I didn't say anything. This whole thing of IT going to the doctor too much had been brewing for a couple of months. A moment later Jackie came out of the nursery and started to take off her coat. My father was standing behind her with his hands on his hips, looking mad.

"Would you please tell me what not acting right means?"

"He just didn't seem right," Jackie said, sounding pretty upset herself. "I can't explain it. It's just something a mother knows."

"Does a mother happen to know what it costs each time she takes Jake to the doctor?" my father fumed.

Jackie glared at him. "I thought it was covered by insurance."

"Some of it is. But when you're going four or five times a month, the part that isn't covered starts to add up."

"Well, maybe I wouldn't have to go as often if I had some help around here," Jackie snapped. "Between taking care of Jake and the house and cooking for you and Kyle, it's just too much. Nobody helps me. You don't even care!"

The next thing we knew she started to sob and ran out of the living room. A second later the bedroom door slammed. My father turned and looked at me wondrously.

"How did we go from taking Jake to the doctor to cleaning the house?" he asked, totally mystified.

What could I say? My father let out a big sigh and started down the hall to the bedroom.

I guess it's like Mr. Orillio said: We all get dealt a hand.

BO

The strangest thing happened Saturday night. I was baby-sitting for Jake Winthrop. It wasn't fun. He's teething and he cries most of the time. Around 9 P.M. a car pulled into the driveway and doors slammed. It was too early for the Winthrops to come home, so I assumed correctly that it was Kyle and Chloe.

They came into the den and we did the awkward hellos. I told them Jake was asleep, and asked if I should go. Kyle started to nod, but Chloe said, "You think he might wake up?"

"It's possible. He's teething."

"She better stay," Chloe said.

The next thing I knew, they went upstairs. I sat there telling myself, *No, this can't be what I think.*

Footsteps upstairs. A door slammed. The argument began. I can only assume neither Kyle nor Chloe realized how thin the walls are.

"This is no good." (Kyle)

"Why?" (Chloe)

"She's here." (Kyle)

"So?" (Chloe)

"So . . . I don't know. It's just weird." (Kyle)

"If it bothers you that much, tell her to go." (Guess who?)

"And what about it?" (I think he meant Jake.)

"What will happen if he wakes up?" (Chloe)

"He'll scream." (Kyle)

They went on like that for a while. Then the door creaked. Two sets of footsteps came down the stairs. Chloe passed without even looking at me. Kyle gave me a little wave. Outside, car doors slammed and the engine started. A screech of rubber in the driveway and the star-crossed couple disappeared into the night.

❖ ❖ ❖

The Winthrops came back from the movies around 11:30. I live about six blocks away so I usually walk home, but it had started to rain so Mr. Winthrop said he'd drive me.

"How's school this year?" he asked in the car as the windshield wipers swished back and forth.

"Fine, Mr. Winthrop. Did Kyle tell you about the play?"

"Play?"

"He didn't tell you he was in the school play?"

Mr. Winthrop glanced at me. "My son Kyle?"

"Uh-oh." I'd spilled the beans.

KYLE

My father and I were watching football. It was Sunday afternoon and Jackie had taken IT to visit her parents. During halftime my father turned to me and said, "You're in a play."

"How'd you find out?"

"Bo, the girl who baby-sits."

"Oh."

"I think it's interesting," he said.

"It's all right."

My father gave me his all-knowing fatherly smile. "It's a step toward something new, Kyle."

"Don't get your hopes up, Dad. I don't think I'm gonna be an actor."

"I wasn't expecting you to," he said. "I'm simply glad that you're finally starting to come out of your shell."

"I was in a shell?" I pretended to be surprised.

"Don't joke. Between me getting married again and your knee, you've been so withdrawn I was worried you'd never come back."

"I'm not so sure I have."

"The acting's a start."

"I was talking about you getting married again," I said.

My father was quiet for a moment. Then his chest heaved. "What happened with your mother was . . ." He shook his head. I'd never really heard him talk about it. It's something neither of us can discuss. "It doesn't mean we stop living, Kyle, even if there are times when we feel like we want to."

I looked back at the halftime show. Mom died. He had a right to marry Jackie. I can't explain what bothered me about it. Something just did.

"You don't have to talk to me about it," my father said. "But it's important that you talk to someone."

"I'm not seeing a shrink," I told him for the billionth time.

"Someone, Kyle."

Sure. Maybe one of the lunch ladies.

BO

Kyle kept giving me looks during rehearsal today. Of course I knew what it had to be about, so when we got to a part where Peter is offstage I went over and said I was sorry.

"Don't tell him anything about me, okay?" he said.

"Your wish is my command," I said.

I thought he'd walk away, but he stayed. We were standing alone in the wing, only a foot apart. His eyes were on me and I felt goose bumps.

"Your face looks thinner," he said.

"So does the rest of me."

"And I'm getting fatter." He pinched a fold of his stomach.

"It doesn't show," I said. Well, maybe it showed just an eensy weensy bit, but who was looking?

"I still eat like I'm in practice six days a

week," he said.

"It must be hard to stop."

"You still swimming?"

"Yes. I haven't seen you there lately."

"It's not my thing," he said.

"Kyle?" Chloe was standing a dozen feet away. I saw surprise in her eyes. As if she was seeing something she hadn't noticed before.

She stepped closer to him. "Can I practice my air raid speech on you?"

"Okay." She and Kyle started to walk away, but as she did, she looked back over her shoulder at me with a curious expression on her face. As if she were thinking, *Is it possible?*

Oddly, I was thinking the same thing.

KYLE

Chloe asked me to come to her house to practice the play today. We've been rehearsing *Anne Frank* for a couple of weeks, working mostly on characterization and blocking. After my knee operation I never thought I'd do any blocking again. Except this kind of blocking means learning where to move onstage.

I got to Chloe's house and she let me in, turning away before I could kiss her, and leading me into the living room.

"Where're your parents?" I asked.

"They went to the city," she said. "I've set things up so that it's like the stage. You can use this as the cat carrier"—she handed me a shoe box, then pointed to a chair—"and we can pretend that's the stove."

I guess she wanted to make it clear that it was all business today.

"Okay." I took off my jacket and got out the playbook.

"We'll start where you take Mouschi out of the carrier."

"Right."

"Go ahead," she said.

I pointed at the playbook. "You're supposed to ask me the cat's name."

"You haven't taken Mouschi out of the carrier," she said.

"Mouschi isn't here."

"Pretend, Kyle. We're rehearsing."

"Okay." So I pretended to take the cat out of the carrier.

"That's not the way you do it," Chloe said.

"Huh?"

"It's your cat, Kyle. You have to treat it like a living thing. If it was a real cat, you wouldn't just take it out of the box and drop it to the floor. You'd gently put it down."

"Well, that's what I'll do."

"Then do it now."

"Here?"

"Yes."

"What's the point?"

"The point is we're rehearsing for a show. You don't rehearse one way and then do it differently when you're onstage."

So I pretended to take invisible Mouschi out of his carrier, gently placed him on the floor, and patted his invisible head. "Nice kitty."

"No," Chloe said.

"Now what?" I asked.

"Don't say 'nice kitty.'"

"What's wrong with *that*?"

"For one thing, it's not in the play. For another, it conveys the wrong mood."

"Mood?"

Chloe gave me this look, like she couldn't believe what a dummy I was. Boy, that pissed me off.

I reached for my jacket. "Look, let's just forget it, okay? I'm already rehearsing this stupid play three hours a day, five days a week. I don't need your help."

"You do, Kyle."

"Says who?"

"Mr. Goodrich."

I stopped and stared at her. "What are you talking about?"

"He asked me to work with you," Chloe said.

"You mean, this was *his* idea?"

"Yes."

"I don't get it."

"He says you need extra help."

"Well, why didn't *he* tell me?" I asked.

"He didn't want to upset you. He's afraid you'll quit."

I stood by the floor-to-ceiling windows and looked out at the water. It was a cold gray day.

The waves had white caps. "Am I that bad?"

"You're inexperienced, Kyle."

"It's just a high school play. I didn't think experience was necessary."

Chloe frowned. "Think of Ben McGillis walking into the middle of a football game."

"He'd get killed."

"Why should a play be any different?"

BO

Today I went to the second career fair in the gym. As I walked past the booths, I sensed a presence following me. It was The Letch. Finally I stopped and confronted him. "I thought you weren't supposed to come to events like this."

"I'm ditching, babe," he said.

I turned around but he continued to follow me, so I stopped at the legal professions booth. The woman there wasn't a lawyer, she was a paralegal. While I talked to her, The Letch stood at the waste management booth next door—rather apt, I thought.

"Is there any way to prevent someone from following you around?" I asked loudly.

"You can have a court order of protection sworn out," the woman said. "But you have to prove that the person is a continuing nuisance."

I turned to The Letch. "Hear that?"

The Letch shrank back into the crowd.

Someone next to me laughed. I turned and found Chloe.

"Is he bothering you?" she asked in a confidential whisper.

"I don't think he can help himself," I whispered back.

Chloe grinned. "It's when he *doesn't* stare at me that I worry."

We started to walk together. Just like that.

"I was in our basement yesterday and found a set of old glasses and a fringed tablecloth," Chloe said. "They must have belonged to my grandparents. Can you use them?"

"Yes!" I exclaimed. "You can't believe how hard it's been to find props like that."

"We have some old chairs, too," she said. "But I'll have to ask my parents."

"Would you? Everything in the prop closet is either un-speakably grungy or broken. We'll take anything you've got."

Chloe stopped. "I know. My basement is full of things I bet you could use. Why don't you come over tonight and we'll go through it together?"

"Uh, okay." Was I hearing her correctly?

"I'm at 4 Bay Street. Know where that is?"

"I have a rough idea," I said.

"It's a dead end and we're the last house. Around eight?"

"Okay."

The bell rang. I could see Chloe's mind skip to her next responsibility. "Great," she said, moving toward the exit. "See you then."

"Chloe?"

She stopped and turned. "Yes?"

"Thanks," I said.

She gave me that winning smile. "Anything for the play, huh?"

In shock, I watched her hurry from the gym. Chloe had just invited me to her *home*?

KYLE

Chloe said everything you say and do onstage sends a message. It's body language. It's the tone of your voice. It really is the way you act. She said the scene with Peter and Anne and the cat isn't about Anne meeting the cat. It's about Peter being shy and withdrawn. My job is to get that message across to the audience.

Acting is a lot harder than I imagined. I really see how I could blow it and look like a fool. So I should quit, right? I mean, there's got to be *someone* at school who can play the role of Peter better than me.

Damn that Chloe. She was right when she said it was hard not to be a hero anymore. Mr. Orillio says it's better to be a has-been than a never-was, but let me tell you, learning to be a has-been ain't easy.

BO

I'm not going to tell you how big Chloe's house is, or how they have this incredible view of the water and a heated pool in their backyard. I'm not going to tell you about all the original art that's hanging on their walls, or how rich I think her parents must be.

But I do wonder how and why she's kept it a secret for so long. I mean we all knew she was well off, but not *that* well off. It's a side of Chloe we've never seen.

Anyway, Chloe and I went through her basement, which is probably larger than my entire house. We pulled sheets off stored furniture and opened dusty cardboard boxes. Just as she'd said, we found sets of plates and glasses and tablecloths and chairs. We picked out what we needed and carried it out to the driveway and packed it into her parents' station wagon.

"I'll drive it to school in the morning and get

Kyle to help me unload it," she said.

"Do you really think you should?" I quickly asked.

"Why not?"

"Doesn't he have a bad knee? Maybe it would be better if I helped you."

"Well, okay."

There was an awkward moment when neither of us was certain what to do next. Chloe looked around and frowned.

"Where's your car?" she asked.

"I don't have one."

"How did you get here?"

"I walked. Anything for the play, remember?"

Chloe smiled. "Come on, I'll give you a ride home."

We got in her car. I don't know what kind it was, but it was a small red convertible and smelled like leather. I gave her directions to my house.

"I'm really glad you changed your mind about stage-managing this production," Chloe said as she drove. "Could you imagine having to deal with someone who didn't know what they were doing?"

"Yes."

Chloe nodded. "Of course. That must be half the people you deal with."

"It *is* a high school production," I said.

Chloe looked at me out of the corner of her eye. "Doesn't that kill you? Why does everyone have this attitude that it has to be unprofessional just because it's high school? Why can't we try to make it the best thing we've ever done?"

"We do," I said. "But there are limits on how much money we have, how much time, and, to be really blunt, how much talent is available."

"I know that, but sometimes I think those limits are used as an excuse not to try."

"I know you feel that way," I said.

Chloe turned into my driveway and stopped. Instead of reaching for the door handle, I just sat there. I felt like she and I had reached a crucial juncture—the central difference in our philosophies toward life in high school.

"I know you don't like me," Chloe said, staring straight ahead as if she couldn't face me.

"I used to not like you," I said. "Now I'm not sure."

She smiled a little. Even in the shadows of the car she had a perfect profile.

"I haven't changed," she said.

"I know."

She hooked her hair behind her ear and looked at me. "You've changed. You've lost weight and bought new clothes. You've done really nice things with your hair."

Yes! I felt like shouting. *Don't you know I'm*

madly in love with your boyfriend?

"I think it's really great," Chloe said.

"Thanks," I said, hating to admit that she sounded sincere.

"Why don't we make this a really great production, Bo?" she said. "This is the last serious play we'll ever do in high school. Why don't we go out with a bang? You and me together."

How could I say no? Nobody *wants* to do a mediocre job, and frankly, I don't think I ever have. But I knew what Chloe meant. I could do a good, competent job, or I could do a *great* job. And why not? Together Chloe and I could make it the best thing we'd ever done.

Chloe and I?

KYLE

Couldn't sleep last night. It's been a long time since that happened to me. For some weird reason I didn't feel like watching TV, so I picked up this book called *North Dallas Forty*. It and *Ball Four* are the only two books I've ever read.

The hero of *North Dallas Forty* is this guy named Phil Elliot, who reveals all this "inside" stuff about professional football. I guess in 1973 when the book came out it must've been a real shock to the football fans of America that these great pro players took drugs off the field to get high and took them on the field to kill the pain so they could play. And I guess it was also shocking that the coach and team management would approve of playing injured and using painkillers. Maybe it was even a shock that players on the same team could hate each other so much and curse each other out.

The thing about *Ball Four* is that it's also

shocking. It's about all the crazy, goofy things a bunch of baseball players did back in the 1960s. But it's also funny and no matter what those guys did, you still get the feeling they loved playing ball and loved being on the team. *North Dallas Forty* makes you feel like Phil Elliot hated the team, hated everything about football except playing the game. He makes the coach and the team owners out to be a bunch of evil cretins who only cared about winning and making money.

I wonder what Phil Elliot would say today, with players earning more than $5 million a year. Everything in sports these days is money. A baseball star making $5 mill a year will sit out the first four or five games of the season and pray his team loses. Why? Because then the owners will give in to his contract demands just to get him back in the lineup. These guys charge $20 for an autograph, and $2,000 an hour to stand around and shake hands at the grand openings of appliance stores.

Team spirit isn't dead. When some guy weeps after losing in the play-offs, it's not just because he won't get a World Series bonus. But the fact that there is a World Series bonus really makes you wonder. It's like nothing's pure anymore. Everything has the taint of money. It used to be the team came first. Now the team may be important, but everyone's looking out for number one, too.

Maybe being in high school is about dreams. About making it big. Almost every guy I know on the football team thinks he's going to the pros. Everyone in the play dreams she or he is headed for Hollywood. Jeff Branco probably hopes he's headed for the FBI's Most Wanted list.

Anne Frank had a dream. She didn't want to be on a professional team, she didn't want a bil-lion-dollar contract. She just wanted to go out-side. She just wanted to walk in the street and look at the sky. How many Anne Franks were there, hiding in attics and basements? Six million Jews died in concentration camps. The Nazis also killed people with mental and physical handi-caps. They all came under the heading of Undesirables.

They all had dreams.

BO

The phone rang tonight. It was Alice. We've both been so busy the last few days that we haven't had time to talk.

"Remember me?" she asked.

"Sorry, I've been distracted. So, how are things on-line?"

"It's over," Alice said. "I've disconnected."

"What? Why?"

"Self-preservation. I was out of control, giving my love away to anyone who could type more than fifteen words a minute. I think I was in love with the idea of being in love."

"What's wrong with that?"

"I was in danger of making romance the central concern of my life," she said. "I almost forgot that I have a life of my own. There's something you must never forget about guys, Bo."

"What's that?"

"They're just guys. They don't make the sun

come up, and they shouldn't change your life."

"I'll remember that," I said.

"So anyway, how are you?"

"Uh, in love."

The phone line grew quiet. I could hear the faint strains of another conversation taking place somewhere in the distance on the information superhighway.

"Hello?" I said.

"I . . . I don't know what to say."

"Join the crowd."

"Does Kyle know?" Alice asked.

"I don't think so."

"Are you feeling okay, Bo?"

"Yes! I'm feeling great! In fact, I can't remember feeling this good."

"All because you're in love with a completely unattainable male who's been going with the same woman for three years and is *still* going with her? I mean, doesn't it seem a little hopeless to you?"

"I'm not thinking about the future," I said.

"That's obvious."

"Why can't you be happy for me?" I asked.

"Because I'm worried," Alice said. "Bobby's worried, too. We think you've either gone completely psycho or you're going to get really hurt."

"What if it's neither?" I asked. "What if it just so happens that Kyle and I enjoy talking and like each other's company?"

"How much time have you spent together?" Alice asked.

"We've talked a few times."

"Oh, Bo . . ." Alice sounded thoroughly disheartened.

"You sound just like my mother before we stopped communicating," I said, getting aggravated. "'Oh, Bo, don't you see what you're getting yourself into?' 'Oh, Bo, how can you do this to yourself?' Oh, Bo, nothing. All my life people have been telling me to take chances. Everyone's always telling me how I never take risks and how I'm too busy trying to protect myself. Now here I'm finally doing something wildly adventurous and everyone I know is trying to protect me."

"Bo, taking risks means learning to skydive or changing the color of your hair."

"Which I did."

"That's the kind of risk you should take."

"But not falling in love with Kyle Winthrop?"

"Be realistic, Bo."

"No."

KYLE

When I got home after rehearsals tonight my father and Jackie were waiting for me in the living room. IT was sitting on the floor chewing on an old red-checked dishrag. Jackie's bought about a hundred different teething toys—rubber pretzels, rings, even something that looks like a dog bone—but IT prefers the rag.

"Have a seat, Kyle," my father said. He looked serious. Jackie looked serious. I felt like I was in court.

"What's up?" I asked.

"Did you tell Jake that Ritz crackers were called soap?" my father asked.

I looked at Jackie. Her eyes were glistening with tears.

"You told him a train was a boat?" my father asked. "And a book was a movie?"

I looked at IT. He had the whole rag in his mouth. His cheeks were bulging and little red and white threads hung out from between his lips.

"Today he kept asking for his boat," Jackie said with a sniff. "Every time I gave it to him he had a tantrum."

"It wasn't a bright idea, Kyle," my father said.

"You might have affected his development," Jackie said.

"It probably won't," my father added. "But you're playing with a small child's mind."

"It's not like I did it on purpose," I said.

"You call it a joke?" Jackie asked, her eyes growing wide.

"I was just fooling around."

My father sighed. "I wish I understood you, Kyle."

BO

Chloe and I went backstage at lunch today. Bobby was there alone, sketching the large panels of canvas that will be the backdrops for the stage. He gave us a wary look, then forced a smile onto his face.

"Hi, Bo, Chloe."

"Hard at work?" I asked.

Bobby's eyes darted around apprehensively. I knew he was wondering what Chloe and I were doing there together.

"Bobby," Chloe said, "we were wondering if we could talk to you about the set."

"What about it?"

"Is there a way that we could make it look more realistic?" I asked.

Bobby put down his pencil and gave us a nervous look. "Like how?"

Chloe and I glanced at each other. We'd talked it over that morning while we unloaded the new props from Chloe's parents' station wagon.

"Suppose instead of drawing windows covered with blackout curtains, we actually had real windows with curtains on them?" I asked.

Bobby winced slightly. "Real *glass* windows?"

"Or just a window frame with the curtains," Chloe quickly added.

"Well, I guess . . ." Bobby said hesitantly.

"And is there any way we could actually use a real bookcase for the secret door?" I asked.

"Instead of a door with a bookshelf painted on it," added Chloe.

"With *real* books?" Bobby's eyebrows rose in horror.

"Maybe you could make some shallow shelves out of wood and draw rows of fake book jackets inside them," Chloe said.

"Well, I guess I could do that," Bobby said. "I mean, I'll have to see what kind of wood we have."

"Maybe some of the guys in the cast could make a bookshelf in wood shop," I said.

"I guess I could ask," Bobby said.

I went over and kissed him on the cheek.

"What's this all about?" Bobby asked.

"It's about going out with a bang," I said.

KYLE

Look, I'm not a sadist. I was just fooling around, okay? There's no way IT is going to turn twelve and still be calling a car a boat or whatever. Lots of kids call things by the wrong names. Then they learn the right names. I'll bet anything if Jackie had already raised a couple of kids this wouldn't have bothered her half as much.

On the other hand, I think Jeff Branco's parents probably have a lot to be worried about. I got into class this morning and all the Pinheads were huddled around the Rat, who was holding a newspaper.

"You gotta see this, Kyle," Lukowsky said. "It's about Jeff. Read it, Peter."

"'A seventeen-year-old man was arrested yesterday for attempting to break into the Fairview Home for Girls,'" the Rat read.

"Wait a minute," I said. "Isn't that the girls' detention home?"

"Yeah."

"'Jeffery Branco, of 243 Oak Avenue, was apprehended inside the facility, which houses young female criminals.'"

"I never heard of anyone trying to break *into* a detention home," said Lukowsky.

The Rat read: "'Police marveled that Branco was able to scale a fifteen-foot chain-link fence topped with razor wire, and pry open a heavily secured door before being discovered in the hallway outside the room of a young woman he claimed was his girlfriend.'"

"Did anybody know he even had a girlfriend?" I asked.

The other Pinheads shook their heads.

"I guess he got really horny," Lukowsky said.

BO

At rehearsal today everyone was talking about Jeff Branco, who might just be the most romantic psychopath since Jack the Ripper. Even Mr. Goodrich was in a good mood.

"Well, it's obvious we should have done Romeo and Juliet this year," he said with a smile.

But his good mood didn't last very long. "All right, everyone," he said, clapping his hands, "let's start from the top of scene three. Peter and Anne, you're sitting at the center table, doing your lessons. It's late in the afternoon and Mr. Frank gives you the signal that you can finally make noise after a long day of silence. Anne playfully takes Peter's shoes, and Peter tries to catch her. Okay? Let's try it."

The scene went all right until the point where Peter shouts, "You're going to be sorry!" and starts to chase Anne. Kyle went after Chloe like a bull through a china shop, knocking over a chair and banging into a table so hard that a glass crashed to the floor. Chloe was supposed to hide behind Cathy Reiner, who plays Mrs. Frank. But Kyle knocked Cathy over and practically tackled Chloe.

"Kyle!" Chloe gasped.

"Ow!" Cathy Reiner sat up, holding her elbow and sobbing.

"Uh, sorry." Kyle offered Cathy a hand, but she looked up at him in terror and backed away. Mr. Goodrich rubbed his face with his hands and shook his head like he was seeing things. "Let's try to remember that we're not on the football field, Kyle."

"Sorry, Mr. G." Kyle looked down and scuffed his shoe against the stage floor. You could see how frustrated and humiliated he was.

"Next time, just *pretend* you're chasing Anne."

"But then it's not going to look real," Kyle said.

Ben McGillis snickered.

"Your job is to make it look real," Mr. Goodrich said. "That's what acting is."

"You'd think he had plenty of experience chasing Chloe," Ben pretended to whisper, but he said it just loud enough for everyone to hear.

Kyle's hands balled into fists and he stormed across the stage toward Ben shouting, "What's *that* supposed to mean?"

Ben backed against a wall and cowered. His eyes darted around in fear as he looked for a way to escape. It looked like Kyle was going to beat him up.

"Kyle, don't!" Chloe and I shouted at the same time and stepped between him and Ben.

Kyle stopped and gave us both a startled look.

Chloe scowled at me.

I realized I'd made a boo-boo.

"Oh, uh, after you," I said.

KYLE

I drove Chloe home after rehearsal tonight. Her car's in the shop and her mom went to the city to meet her father for a show. She hardly said a word.

"Something wrong?" I asked.

She glanced at me. Her eyes said something was wrong, but her mouth said nothing.

"You think I'm wrecking the play?" I asked.

"I really don't want to talk about it."

"Why not?"

No answer. I pulled into her driveway and she started to reach for the door handle. Suddenly she stopped.

"What is it?" I asked.

"The front door."

The house was dark and the front door was wide open.

"We'd better call the police," she said.

"Wait, Chloe, maybe your mom left it open. There're no cars around."

"But someone could be inside."

"If anyone was going to rob your house, I doubt they'd leave the door open."

"You think?" Chloe seemed uncertain.

"Let's check it out." I started to get out of the car.

We walked up the path and peeked inside. Chloe reached in and turned on the hall and living room lights. Nothing looked disturbed.

"This is weird," she said, pointing at the keypad on the wall that ran the alarm system. "It's not even on."

"Your mom was probably in a rush," I said.

"It's not like her. She's usually super careful."

At Chloe's insistence, we searched every room and every closet, plus the attic, basement, and garage. By the time we finished, every light in the house was burning.

"I think it's okay," I said as we stood in the front hall.

Chloe bit her lower lip and hugged herself. "I don't feel safe, Kyle."

"Want me to stay until your parents come home?"

I could almost see the gears in Chloe's mind spinning. Who would've thought it would be such a big deal for me to stay a couple of hours?

"Okay, Kyle."

It was late and we hadn't eaten so Chloe ordered in a pizza for me and a salad for herself. We sat in the kitchen. Chloe picked at her salad.

She seemed tense, like she didn't know what I would do or say. I knew she felt trapped and I didn't want her to feel uncomfortable, so I just said the first thing that came into my mind. "What do you like about acting?"

Chloe gave me this look, like why would I ask *that*?

"I'm serious," I said.

"I . . . I think I like pretending I'm someone else."

"Why?"

"It's an escape," she said. "A relief from being me."

"Huh?" I'd never heard her say anything like that before.

"There's another part of it," Chloe added quickly, as if she regretted what she'd just said and wanted to get past it fast. "I like the idea that everybody's watching me, and that if I'm doing it well I can move them emotionally. I can make them laugh or cry. And sometimes, if I'm really good, I can make them love me."

"That's what you want? For everyone to love you?"

Chloe picked a sliver of onion out of her salad and bit it. "I never thought about it that way, but yes, I probably do." She paused. "I mean, isn't that what everybody wants?"

"I'd settle for just one person," I said.

BO

It's amazing how fast time passes. Dress rehearsals are suddenly two weeks away.

I was in the prop closet behind the stage today. Chloe and I want to find the most authentic-looking suits and dresses possible. Mr. Goodrich said there might be some old things in the closet so I went to take a look. The prop closet is big, dusty, and dark with lots of old props and backdrops leaning against the walls. I couldn't find the light switch so I left the door open to let the light in.

I was digging through old sofas, papier-mâché trees, and assorted junk when the room suddenly grew dimmer. I spun around and saw a silhouette standing in the doorway.

"Who is it?" I asked, gripped by a sudden nervousness.

"Lookin' good, babe." It was The Letch.

"What are you doing here?" I felt my breath

grow short as a number of truly unpleasant scenarios raced through my mind.

"Just lookin' for some lights."

"Wouldn't they be in the electrical closet?" I asked.

"I figured I'd check here, too," he said.

"You know they're not here. Can't you think of anything better to do than follow me around?"

"Sure, I can think of something better to do. Interested?" He started to close the door behind him.

I felt my heart start to pound. "Have you ever heard me scream? It's really quite an experience."

"Hey, lighten up." The Letch let go of the door. "I was only foolin' around."

"Go fool around in someone else's closet," I told him.

Then The Letch did the most shocking thing. His shoulders sagged and he said, "How come you're always so mean to me?"

I was utterly dumbfounded. Could it be that under that dumb lecherous exterior lurked a dumb but sensitive human being? Suddenly I felt terrible.

"I really don't mean to be such a crab," I told him softly. "I just don't want you to get the wrong idea."

"Maybe *you're* the one with the wrong idea," he said. "I mean, how do you know what I'm like if you won't even give me a chance?"

He was right. I wouldn't give him a chance. But that was beside the point. What could I say that would both convince him that I wasn't interested while at the same time not hurt his feelings any more than I already had?

It was at that precise moment that the door swung open. Kyle stood there with a startled look on his face.

"Oh, uh, sorry, didn't mean to interrupt." He began to back out.

"You weren't!" I gasped. Talk about people getting the wrong idea! I quickly grabbed The Letch by the arm and led him out of the closet. "We'll talk about it later, okay?"

"Uh . . . sure." The Letch sounded surprised. "I'll call you tonight."

"Yes, do that." *Do anything, I thought, but just go!*

The Letch went. I turned to Kyle and smiled. "Hi."

"Hi. You sure I wasn't interrupting?"

"Karl and I? No, no. We were just discussing the lighting."

Kyle frowned. "In a dark closet?"

"Well, as a matter of fact, we were discussing the lighting in this closet," I ad-libbed. "I can never find anything in here because it's so dark."

"All you have to do is turn on the switch." He

reached toward the wall and the closet filled with light.

"Will you look at that! I never knew it was there!" Rarely have I felt like more of a complete idiot.

"You usually find light switches near the door," he said in a teasing tone.

It was clearly time to change the subject. "So what are you doing back here anyway?"

"Mr. G said you might need some help moving stuff," Kyle said.

"That was thoughtful of him."

Kyle moved things out of the way so I could look for old costumes. There's something wonderful about being near an attractive male who is moving heavy objects. You can almost feel his strength. Kyle was wearing a T-shirt and I watched his arm muscles flex and unflex. I couldn't help thinking how wonderful it would be if someone came along and turned off the light and closed the door . . . and then Kyle took me in his arms.

KYLE

I was watching an international kite-flying competition on the tube when Jackie came into the den.

"Can we talk?"

Uh-oh. Sounded like trouble. I lowered the volume with the remote. Jackie sat down with this little plastic walkie talkie she carries around so she can listen in on IT while he's napping in his crib.

"I've never had a teenaged stepson before," she said, nervously twisting a hair band in her fingers. "But I think it's time we talked, Kyle. I'm very upset about what happened with Jake. I feel that what you did was a hostile act that was really directed at me. . . . Can you see that?"

I'm not big on all this psychology stuff, but for the sake of avoiding an argument I sort of tipped my head up and down to indicate "yes."

"Honestly, Kyle, I've tried very hard to make

this work, but I don't feel that you're trying at all. In fact, all I feel from you is hostility. You constantly avoid me, you won't talk, you've made it clear I'm not to enter your room."

I sort of shrugged "Could be."

"I've talked this over with your father. He's agreed that maybe you and I should go see someone together."

"You mean a shrink?" I asked. "You and me?"

"It's called family counseling."

Who cared what it was called? She may have been married to my father, but I've never spent more than five minutes alone with her.

"Let's wait a day and see what happens," I said.

Jackie's jaw dropped. Then she gave me a knowing smirk. "Couldn't you come up with something a little more original?"

BO

I arrived at the auditorium early for rehearsals today.

Once again I've reached that point in the production where it feels like I spend more time in this approximation of a theater than I do in my own home. I was walking across the stage when I heard someone clear his throat.

"Ahem."

I looked up. Bobby and Alice were sitting on the catwalk.

"Look who's here," Bobby said.

"I remember her," said Alice.

"She probably doesn't remember us," said Bobby.

"What do you expect?" Alice asked. "She's a redhead now."

"Auburn," I said.

"Notice her new attitude?" Alice said.

"Reminds me of Chloe," said Bobby.

"I thought she hated Chloe," said Alice.

"That was before," said Bobby. "Now they're best friends."

"Wrong," I said.

"She says we're wrong," Bobby said.

"I hope so," said Alice. "Because Chloe Frost becomes friends with people so she can use them to get what she wants."

"What could she possibly want from Bo?" Bobby asked with feigned innocence.

"She wants to make *Anne Frank* the best production this school's ever seen," I said.

"How noble!" Alice gasped.

"How selfless!" cried Bobby.

"How amazingly bogus," Alice grumbled.

"It's not," I said. "It's true."

"She says it's true," said Bobby.

My neck was starting to ache from looking up at them.

"How's Kyle?" Alice asked.

"Okay, I guess."

"Notice she acts like she hardly knows him?" Bobby said.

"That's true," I said.

"Didn't you tell me you were in love?" Alice asked.

"All Kyle and I do is talk," I said.

"Think Chloe's noticed?" Bobby asked.

"That girl doesn't miss a trick," said Alice.

"You don't think Chloe's gotten friendly with Bo so that she can keep tabs on what's going on with Kyle, do you?" Bobby asked.

"That's absurd," I said.

"She says it's absurd," Alice said.

"If Chloe thought there was anything between Kyle and me she'd do just the opposite," I said, rubbing my neck. "She'd hate me."

"Not Chloe," said Alice.

"She's too smart," said Bobby.

"All right," I said. "Can I ask *you guys* a question?"

"What do you think?" Bobby asked Alice.

"Let's hear it, then decide," Alice replied.

"What does Chloe Frost see in Kyle Winthrop?" I asked.

"I think the more interesting question is, what do *you* see in him, Bo," answered Bobby.

"No fair," I said. "I asked first."

"She's right." Alice gave in. "Okay, here's what I think. Chloe Frost has to be the best at whatever she does. And that includes having boyfriends. When Kyle Winthrop was captain of the football team, he was the best boyfriend a girl could have, so Chloe had to have him."

"You really think she's that shallow?" I asked.

"Deep down we're all that shallow," Bobby said.

"Ha-ha," I said.

"Maybe not shallow," Alice said. "Driven. I don't think she can help herself."

"And now that Kyle's not captain of the football team?" I asked.

"Chloe's facing a dilemma," Bobby said. "It's been apparent to Chloe watchers lately that she's really not interested in him anymore. But at the same time, she can't face the idea that he was simply a possession. She doesn't want to believe that she's that superficial."

"Deep down we're all that superficial," Alice said.

"Do I hear an echo?" asked Bobby.

"Then what's going to happen?" I asked. Despite the rubbing, my neck continued to throb.

"Bo's asking us to predict," Alice said.

"Sorry, we're not prognosticators," Bobby said.

"Oh, go on." Alice nudged him. "Take a wild guess."

"You sure?" Bobby asked.

"Why not?"

"Okay, here's a possible scenario," Bobby said. "Chloe and Kyle break up; Kyle finds another girlfriend; Chloe starts dating a guy from college; neither talks to Bo again."

"What do you think of that?" Alice asked, looking down at me.

"I think talking to you guys is getting to be a real pain in the neck," I said.

KYLE

I was standing in the kitchen this morning, eating out of a box of strawberry Post Toasties, when IT waddled in clutching a disposable plastic razor with the cover off.

"Wha dis?" he asked, holding it up.

I had this vision of him trying to imitate me or my father shaving, except IT would probably lop off an entire layer of skin and maybe some baby fat, too.

So I bent down, grabbed his pudgy little wrist, and started to twist the razor out of his hand. "It's a razor," I said. "Not for little kids. Very, very dangerous. Understand?"

"Mine!" IT clenched the razor with all his might, like he wasn't going to let go unless I chopped his hand off.

"You have to give it to me," I said.

"Mine, mine!" he shouted again as I slowly pried the razor out of his grip. I couldn't believe how strong the kid was.

"You can't play with it." I finally got the razor out of his hand. I figured he'd go bawling to Jackie and make a real stink. But instead of crying, he just stared up at me with this amazed look on his face, as if he'd never heard my voice before. And I was looking down at this drooling toothless wonder and thinking what a tough, stubborn little guy he was.

And then it struck me. This is my half brother. Maybe it's not so surprising.

BO

Last night the phone rang. My heart leapt into my throat. Was it Kyle? Calling to arrange a secret tryst? I raced to the phone and answered it with a breathless, "Hello?"

"Uh, hi, Bo."

It wasn't Kyle. "Who is this?" I asked.

"Uh, it's Karl."

"Karl?" For a moment the name meant nothing.

"Yeah, Karl, your friendly techie and AV dude."

The memory of that afternoon in the prop closet bounced back like a bad check. He said he'd call.

"Oh, God, Karl," I gasped. "You really caught me at a bad time. I'll have to call you back later."

I hung up, depressed.

KYLE

More news about Jeff Branco. Turns out his girl-friend went to a school across town called Portswell High. About two months ago she was sent to Fairview after she got into a razor fight with another girl and cut her up pretty bad. Sounds like a sweet kid, huh?

According to the paper, the reason Jeff broke into Fairview was to give her a present. The police said they found a jewelry box in his pocket and inside was an expensive solid gold heart-shaped locket with a picture of him.

I bet that's why Jeff was selling pizza in the boys' room. He was saving up money for that gold locket. I kind of wish I'd known Jeff Branco better. I mean, I always thought he was just your average run-of-the-mill headcase. Now it's obvious the kid has depth.

BO

I feel like singing! On Saturday night I went to Kyle's house to baby-sit. Jackie said Jake had taken a long nap that afternoon and would probably stay up late. I wasn't thrilled by the news. I'd rented *A Star Is Born* with Judy Garland, but it appeared that I'd be watching reruns of *Sesame Street* instead.

Just as Jake and I settled in front of the television, I heard footsteps coming down the stairs. For a moment I was terrified that someone had broken in through an upstairs window, but then Kyle appeared.

"Hi," he said.

"Hi," I said, noticing that he was wearing navy blue sweatpants and a white sweatshirt, not exactly the clothes he wore for dates with Chloe.

"Did they leave?" he asked.

"About five minutes ago."

"Jackie didn't say anything about dinner, did she?"

"Not to me."

Just then Jake pointed at the TV and said, "Wha dis?"

Both Kyle and I looked. It was a *Sesame Street* segment on pizza, and we watched the man on the screen toss the dough in the air and catch it, then spread the tomato sauce and cheese on it.

"It's pizza," Kyle said.

"Peet," Jake said.

"Hey, Jake," Kyle said. "How'd you like to see a pizza in real life?"

Jake looked at him with the cutest little confused expression on his face. I suspect I looked somewhat confused, too, since it was probably the first time I'd ever seen Kyle talk to his half brother.

"What do you say we go to the mall and have some real pizza?" Kyle said.

"You're going to take Jake?" I asked, surprised.

"Sure, why not?"

"Should I wait here until you get back?" I asked.

Now it was Kyle's turn to look confused. "Of course not," he said. "We'll all go."

Does that qualify as a date?

❖   ❖   ❖

Please don't laugh. But pushing Jake in the stroller with Kyle by my side was like . . . well, it was like being married.

Sure, sure, I know I have an active fantasy

life, but still, Kyle did take us for pizza and we did cut a slice into tiny pieces to feed to Jake, who managed to smear red sauce over 90 percent of his face. Then Kyle decided to get his car cleaned so we accompanied him to the car wash. I didn't mind. I would've gone anywhere with him.

I kept thinking what a scandal it would be if anyone we knew from school saw us, but no one did. Of course I was dying to ask him where Chloe was. But I didn't. At least not until we got back to his house. By then Jake had fallen asleep so I changed his diaper and put him in the crib. Meanwhile Kyle made a big bowl of popcorn. Then we met in the den.

"Can I show you something?" he asked.

"Uh, sure," I said, a little uncertainly, wondering what he had in mind.

Kyle turned on the TV and slid a cassette into the VCR. The next thing I knew, I was looking at something resembling roast beef on a white bread roll underwater. A tiny worm-like thing was gnawing away at the roast beef, and little flecks of red quickly floated away with the current.

"What is this?" I asked.

"My knee," Kyle said.

"Excuse me?"

"That's the inside of my knee."

"Huh? How?"

"Arthroscopic surgery," Kyle explained.

"They use a little TV camera to look inside the knee. The surgeon watches the whole thing on a monitor while he works with these tiny instruments."

"But the water …"

"That's how he can see. They flush the knee with sterile water."

"What's the ragged red stuff?"

"Torn cartilage," Kyle said, munching on a handful of popcorn. "He's cutting it away. In a second he's gonna get to the ligament."

He offered me some popcorn.

"Uh, no thanks," I said.

"You're not grossed out, are you?"

"Not exactly."

"I can turn it off."

"Has Chloe ever seen this?" I asked.

"She wouldn't watch."

"Leave it on," I said.

◇ ◇ ◇

Around midnight Brian and Jackie came home.

"Okay, Bo, get your coat," Brian said.

Then Kyle said, "I'll drive her."

I couldn't believe it. I kept thinking, *This isn't happening to me. It's happening to someone else.*

Kyle and I went out to his car and got in.

"Can I ask you a question?" I said.

"Okay."

"Do you show that tape to a lot of people?"

"No."

"Was there some reason why you wanted me to see it?"

Kyle gave one of his characteristic shrugs. "I don't know. I just thought you could appreciate it."

A little while later he pulled into my driveway. I wished I lived six hundred miles away instead of six blocks so we could have spent all night in the car just driving and talking. I looked through the windshield and saw the curtain in the living room move slightly.

"I think someone's watching us," Kyle said.

"My mom."

"Guess you better go in."

I felt my heart sink, but he was right.

"Well, thanks. I had fun tonight," I said.

"Me, too."

I waited for a second longer, just in case. But nothing happened. I reached for the door handle.

"Bo?" Kyle said.

"Yes?"

"Do I really suck as an actor?"

I knew it must have taken a lot of courage for him to ask that. "No. And the more you rehearse, the better you'll get."

"We've been rehearsing for nearly two months," he said.

He was right. We sat in the car, in the shadows cast by the street light. Kyle was asking me to be honest. How can you be honest with someone you're madly, passionately in love with?

I decided to take a chance. His right hand was resting on the seat between us and I slid my hand over it. Kyle looked down at our hands and then up at me. He didn't try to pull his hand away.

"You're five times better than you were two months ago," I said. "You're comfortable with the material now. You know what to do. I can't tell you that you'll win an Academy Award someday, Kyle, but you'll do fine in this play."

"Promise?"

"Promise." I squeezed his hand, and couldn't believe what a liar I'd become.

KYLE

Today in Pinhead homeroom Mr. Orillio wrote a message in big letters on the blackboard:

CHANGE YOUR ATTITUDE
TO GRATITUDE

It reminded me that I'm a seventeen-year-old has-been. Then I thought about Peter Van Daan, who probably would have been a never-was if it hadn't been for Anne Frank. A lot of people in Europe during World War II never even got to be has-beens just because they were in the wrong place at the wrong time.

I guess I'm supposed to feel lucky that I'm alive, and well fed, and a free person living in the United States, instead of starving under some dictatorship in Africa or someplace.

But sometimes it's hard to feel that way. Especially when you're seventeen, and you've destroyed your knee and you can't do the one thing you really love.

Sometimes I just feel like life sucks.

Then I catch myself and wonder what good being bummed out does?

Guess I'm trying to change my attitude.

BO

Bobby and I made the rounds with the recycling cart again today.

"If I talk about Kyle, will it make you angry?" I asked.

"Probably."

"Please, Bobby, I have to talk to *someone*."

"Oh, all right."

"I think it's getting serious," I said.

Bobby studied me for a second. "Why?"

"He let me watch the tape of his knee operation."

"*What?*"

I explained about the tiny camera going inside Kyle's knee.

"So why does that make it serious?" Bobby asked.

"He gave me a glimpse of what's inside."

Bobby stopped the cart. "Bo, are you feeling okay?"

"Giddy."

"I'll say."

"Wait, it gets stranger. I feel like Chloe and I are really becoming friendly."

"I wouldn't count on being friendly with her for too long," Bobby warned.

"I know," I said. "But isn't it fascinating? I mean, who could have imagined Kyle, Chloe, and I, thrown together in a complex triangle of human emotions?"

"You've been watching too many soap operas," Bobby said, and started pulling the cart again.

The funny thing is I don't watch any. Who needs to watch when you're living one?

KYLE

Mr. Orillio was taking attendance when the door opened and Jeff Branco stepped in. I almost didn't recognize him. He was wearing a new pair of jeans and a fresh blue shirt. The bandanna and black leather vest were gone.

We all stood up and applauded.

"All right, Jeff!"

"Way to go, dude!"

"Welcome back, dirtbag."

Mr. Orillio even shook Jeff's hand. "Jeff, I don't usually condone acts of criminality, but I wanted to congratulate you on the sheer originality of your plan. You may be the first person in history to actually break *into* prison just to give your girlfriend her birthday present."

The Rat raised his hand. "Can we ask questions, Mr. O?"

"It's up to Jeff," Mr. Orillio said. Jeff said okay. Next thing we knew, it was show-and-tell.

The Rat went first. "What's your current legal status?"

"I'm out on bail," Jeff explained. "I would've come back sooner, but the lawyer put me in this mental hospital so I could see some shrinks. He said it'll help get me a reduced sentence."

"How come you didn't just wait until visiting hours to see your girlfriend?" Lukowsky asked.

"See, that's where the newspapers really screwed up," Jeff said. "I didn't break into Fairview just because it was Mindy's birthday. It was because it was her birthday and her stupid parents told the 'authorities' I wasn't allowed to see her no more."

"Why not?" Peter asked.

"They said I was a bad influence," Jeff said. "I mean, their daughter slices some other chick into Wonder Bread, and they think *I'm* the bad influence?"

Go figure.

BO

Today was Set Day—the day everyone pitches in and finishes painting and building the set. And that meant I'd be working shoulder to shoulder with The Letch, who was probably wondering why I'd never returned his call. So I went down to the AV room.

A gremlin wearing thick glasses and a Jimi Hendrix T-shirt opened the door. The room was filled with loud Grateful Dead music and body odor. "A lady! Please come in."

"I came to talk to Karl," I said, hesitating before I entered. "Is everyone decent?"

"I think so," said the gremlin. "Hey! Turn down the music, phlegmwads. There's a lady here to see Karl."

A few moments later Karl appeared from behind the gray metal shelves. He didn't look happy to see me.

"What's up, Bo?"

I held out my hand. "Can we just be friends?"

The Letch looked at my hand and then at me. "That's all?"

"Sorry."

The Letch looked disappointed, but he shook my hand anyway.

"Thanks," I said, grateful that he understood. For an instant I considered kissing him on the cheek . . . but then I thought better of it.

◊   ◊   ◊

Later we all got together and finished the set. Chloe always finds a way to avoid getting her hands dirty, and today was no exception. She said she wasn't feeling well and went home.

By 9 P.M. the set was finished and everyone had started to leave. Soon, only Bobby, Alice, Mr. Goodrich, Kyle, and I were left.

"Need a ride?" Bobby asked from the aisle.

I was sitting on the edge of the stage, making some changes in the cue notes. "Go ahead," I said. "I still have some things to do."

"It's late, Bo," Bobby said. "How are you going to—"

He didn't finish the sentence. I turned around and saw that Kyle had just come out from backstage, carrying a paint bucket and some brushes.

Bobby forced a weak smile onto his face. "I get it, Bo. Don't do anything I wouldn't do." Then he turned and left.

I watched him go and then looked back at Kyle. "Almost finished?"

"I just want to wash these brushes out in the sink," he said, and headed toward the janitor's room.

No sooner had he left, then Mr. Goodrich appeared.

"I guess that's it, Bo," he said. "Ready to go?"

"Kyle's in the janitor's room," I said.

Mr. Goodrich looked at his watch and frowned. "I told Dory I'd be home half an hour ago."

"Go ahead," I said. "I'll lock up." As stage manager I was one of the few students in school allowed to have a key.

"Well, all right, don't stay too late."

Mr. Goodrich walked up the aisle and through the auditorium doors. Suddenly, it was very quiet. The only sound was water splashing in the sink of the janitor's room as Kyle washed the brushes.

I took a deep breath and let it out slowly. My heart was drumming. I was about to do something I'd never done before. I was tired of waiting for Kyle to make the first move. Tonight I was going to force the issue.

The sound of splashing water stopped. A door creaked. I could hear the faintest pad of tennis shoes on the floor. My heart was racing even faster than before and my throat felt tight. *Don't chicken out, I told myself. You have a right to know what he's thinking.*

Kyle came through the door and walked along the auditorium floor in front of the stage.

"I left the brushes in the greenroom to dry," he said. He stopped and looked around. "Where is everyone?"

"They've gone."

Kyle stopped a few feet from me and leaned his elbow on the stage. "What a day, huh?"

"It seemed like it would never end," I said.

"Kind of scary," Kyle said.

"Why?"

"The set's done. Rehearsals are almost over. Dress rehearsals start next week. I mean, this whole thing is real. It's really gonna happen."

"You'll be fine, Kyle."

Kyle smiled. "How come you always know what I'm thinking?"

Could you ask for a better opening?

I slid over until I was close to him. "Maybe we're on the same wavelength."

We were barely inches apart now. Kyle looked up into my eyes. Searchingly? I wondered. Was he realizing that I could give him the love and devotion Chloe was too busy to spare?

"Bo, I—" he started to say.

"Don't," I said, leaning toward him.

I closed my eyes and kissed him on the lips. I thought it was the bravest thing I'd ever done.

It wasn't a long kiss. When I opened my eyes, Kyle was staring past me at something. I turned my head and saw the silhouette of someone standing in the doorway at the far end of the auditorium.

She backed away and let the door swing closed.

"Chloe!" Kyle shouted.

The next thing I knew, he ran up the aisle and out the auditorium door.

❖   ❖   ❖

I don't know how long I sat there. I don't know if I really believed Kyle would come back for me. After a while the auditorium door did open. Bobby stuck his head in.

"Bo? You okay?"

I knew if I answered, I'd burst into tears. So I just shook my head.

"I called your house and your mom said you weren't home yet," Bobby said, stepping into the auditorium. "Want a ride?"

I slid off the stage and started to walk up the aisle. Bobby held the door open for me.

"Aren't we supposed to lock it?" he asked as we went out the front door.

I handed him the key and Bobby did the honors.

Then we went to his car and he drove me home.

Neither of us said a word until he stopped in my driveway. I felt tears falling out of my eyes, but I wasn't blubbering.

"How did you know I was there?" I asked with a sniff. "I mean, how did you know I wasn't off parking somewhere with Kyle locked in a passionate embrace?"

"Don't do this to yourself," Bobby said softly.

I glared at him, but the anger melted away. It wasn't his fault.

"Can you take me someplace?" I asked.

"Not Kyle's, I hope."

"No. 7-Eleven."

KYLE

All this time I thought Bo was just being friend-ly. Like we were teammates on the theater team. I mean, sure we had some nice talks, and we took IT out for pizza that night, but I didn't think I was leading her on in any way. Unless she thought watching my knee operation was a romantic come on.

I felt crummy. I mean, Bo was the one person in the play I could be comfortable and relaxed with. *Whoa!* you're probably thinking, what about Chloe?

You think I could feel comfortable and relaxed with her?

Give me a break.

So here's a question for you philosophers out there: What is love? Is love selling pizza in the boys' room so you can buy a gold locket for your girlfriend? Is it breaking into a girls' house of detention to give it to her? Or is it being with someone just so you know you'll always have a date on Saturday night?

BO

I was sitting on the catwalk, scarfing down a box of Ring Dings, when I heard footsteps.

"Is she back there?" Alice asked.

"No," replied Bobby. "Check out front."

Alice walked directly beneath me and peered out into the empty auditorium. "Not there either."

She was joined by a head full of gorgeous blond dreadlocks. "I know she came to school this morning."

I ripped open a new Ring Ding. Alice and Bobby both looked up.

"Home sweet home," said Bobby.

"I feel like I never left," I said.

"Chloe quit, you know," said Alice.

"What!?" I looked down at them in utter disbelief.

"She walked into Mr. G's room this morning and resigned."

"Why?" I asked.

"We thought you'd know."

"Did something happen last night?" Alice asked.

"She won," I said.

Alice gave me a puzzled look. "Does this have something to do with Kyle?"

My eyes met Bobby's. "I didn't know if you wanted me to tell her," he said.

"Everything," I said.

A door squeaked and I heard heavier footsteps. Mr. Goodrich stepped onto the stage and looked up at me. "I thought you'd given up the catwalk."

"It was only a temporary thing."

"What are we going to do?" he asked.

"Beth Villeta's her understudy," I said.

Mr. Goodrich crossed his arms and tried to look stern. "I want you to talk to Chloe, Bo."

"Why me?"

"Because you've been the closest to her this last month. Try to change her mind."

"This ought to be good," Bobby muttered.

"What?" Mr. Goodrich asked, puzzled.

"Chloe and I have had, er, a personal difference," I said.

"More like a personal similarity, if you ask me," quipped Alice.

"No one asked you," I said.

"This is shaping up to be a disaster," Mr. Goodrich groaned.

"Maybe," I said. "But the show must go on."

KYLE

The girl who played Meip is now playing Anne. Maybe I'm not the worst actor in the group anymore. Actually, I'm probably still the worst, but at least I know my lines. Not being the worst doesn't make me feel any better, though. We all know the play is no good without Chloe.

I tried to talk to her that night after she saw Bo and me in the auditorium, but it was no use. She didn't want to listen.

All she said was, "I wish you still played football."

BO

We had the first run-through today. It was death. I've never seen a more depressed group of people. Beth Villeta was incredibly courageous, stepping into the Anne part just four days before the preview. But it's hopeless. There simply isn't enough time to learn the lead role.

After the run-through, Bobby, Alice, and I sat in the front row of the auditorium, staring at the stage.

"It's a beautiful set," I said sadly.

"Thanks," said Bobby. "Your suggestions really helped. It took a lot of extra work, but it was worth it."

"*Would have been* worth it," Alice corrected him.

"Anyway, they were mostly Chloe's ideas," I said.

"I hate to say this," Bobby said with regret, "but I really do think she made us better than we thought we could be."

"I think back to all those productions where Chloe drove us crazy," I said. "All those times I prayed she'd fall off the stage and break both legs. Now she's quit and it's a nightmare."

Alice slumped down in her seat. "She's just being spiteful."

"I think she feels betrayed," I said. "She tried so hard, and all we did was snake her boyfriend."

"What's this *we* stuff?" Alice asked.

"She's right, Bo," Bobby said.

They were both staring at me. I shrank down in my seat. "Okay, so I made a mistake. What can I do about it now?"

"Make it right," Bobby said.

KYLE

I came out of the lunch line and headed for the team table. Alex Gidden and Jason Rooney were already there.

"Where's Eddie?" I asked as I put down my tray.

Alex pointed over to the window. Eddie was sitting by himself in the corner, hunched over with his head in his hands. "What's goin' on?" I asked.

"The big enchilada went bye-bye," Jason said.

"Nothing?" It was hard to believe no school had offered him a scholarship.

"Zippo. Nada."

I went over and sat down next to him. He glanced at me and stared back down at the floor. Not even a "Hi, bro."

"It sucks, man," I said.

Eddie's head bobbed up and down. "Tell me about it. Not one lousy offer. Not even from one of those cheesy division three schools in the Midwest."

"Are you sure you've heard from everyone?"

"Yeah."

"It doesn't make sense, man. Someone was going to take you. All those scouts who came to watch. They wouldn't have wasted their time."

"A couple called," Eddie said. "They said I came real close and they were sorry."

Eddie and I both stared at the floor.

"It was gonna be you and me, man," he said sadly. "We were the stars. We were gonna bite the big enchilada, get the four-year rides. Now look at us. A couple of losers."

I winced. The word stung. Not me, I thought. I'm not a loser.

"What're you gonna do?" I asked.

"Who knows?" Eddie chewed on his thumb. "Get a job, go to some community college. . . . It doesn't matter. I'm off the pro track. Wherever I go, no one's gonna see me. No one's gonna scout me. It's over. The whole thing was a bust, a total waste."

"Hey, we had some great times." I tried to cheer him up.

Eddie glanced at me angrily. "Who gives a crap?"

"I'm just saying it wasn't a total waste," I said. "We were out there. We were *feared*. Maybe it's over now, but we'll always have that. I mean, we'll always know we once ruled."

Eddie gazed up at me with this look of disbelief on his face. "What are you talking about?"

"I'm talking about what we were. We were it. Better to be a has-been than a never-was."

"Get lost," he mumbled.

"I'm serious."

"I said, get lost!" Eddie gave me a shove.

I got to my feet and almost hit him, but I knew it was dumb. Eddie glanced at me and growled, "Go do your stupid play."

I wanted to tell him that it might have been stupid, but it sure beat wallowing in self pity. Instead I went back to the table.

Alex looked up at me. "Eddie's really bummed."

"It's like his whole life is down the tubes," said Jason.

The other guys nodded in agreement. They were all sitting there with their shoulders sagging and their heads down. Suddenly I felt like I was at a funeral. Did someone die?

"What are you guys talking about?" I asked. "It's only football."

They looked at me with shocked expressions on their faces like I'd broken some religious taboo or something.

Next thing I knew, I picked up my tray and

walked away, not even sure where I was going. I stopped in the middle of the cafeteria, and looked around for a place to sit.

"Yo, Kyle!" Someone waved from the table right in front of me. It was Lukowsky. The Rat, Branco, and some of the other Pinheads were all watching.

"Lookin' for a place to sit?" Lukowsky asked.

"Shut up," The Rat snapped at him. "You know he ain't gonna sit with us."

Lukowsky stared down at his lunch, and the other guys looked away. *The Undesirables . . .*

Think about it . . .

"Make room, you goofballs." I sat down.

BO

It's funny how I knew exactly where to find Chloe between classes. She was hiding in a stall in the girls' room. As I stood staring at her Weejuns under the stall wall, I kept thinking, *Why does Chloe need to hide?*

The bell rang and the girls' room cleared out. I waited by the mirror. Finally the stall door opened. Chloe stepped out and froze. Then she gathered herself together and started to go past me.

"I think we should talk," I said, positioning myself between her and the door.

"There's nothing to talk about."

"There's lots to talk about."

"Please get out of my way."

"No."

Chloe glared at me. "So, in addition to changing our hair and losing weight, we're now taking assertiveness training? I should have guessed. How else would you have gotten up the nerve to try to steal my boyfriend?"

"I didn't try to steal him."

"Oh, please." Chloe rolled her eyes in fine dramatic tradition.

"At least, not consciously," I said. "And anyway, it doesn't really seem like you want him anymore."

Except for the hissing of steam from the radiator, the bathroom became quiet. The bell had rung and in classrooms all around us our fellow students were facing another forty-two minutes of torture. Meanwhile, Chloe and I dawdled in the aromatic netherworld of the girls' room.

"Everything's so complicated." Chloe's shoulders slumped. She checked her Swatch. "Oh, God, I'm late!"

"What's your next class?" I asked.

"Calculus."

"Skip it?"

Chloe's eyes widened. "Bo, I've never . . ."

"Then it's about time."

❖   ❖   ❖

We wound up sitting on the catwalk with our feet hanging in the air and our arms resting on the low railing. Chloe was uncharacteristically quiet.

"Ring Ding?" I offered her one of my chocolate-covered delicacies.

Chloe unwrapped it and took a small bite. "I

hate it," she said with a dainty sigh.

"The Ring Ding?" I asked.

"No, everything else. You'll never believe this, Bo, but I *despise* competition."

"You're right, I'll never believe it."

"The only thing I hate worse is losing."

"*That* I believe."

Chloe took another bite and licked a little piece of chocolate off her glossy lips. "Competing is simply the lesser of two evils. I've never joined a team. All my activities are noncompetitive."

"You always have to be the best," I said.

"Is that really so bad?"

"No. It's . . . just that sometimes, it seems a little . . . compulsive."

Chloe studied her perfectly manicured fingernails. "My father's a plastic surgeon. No one wants a 'just okay' nose job. Everyone wants the perfect nose. There's no room for anything less."

"Why did you quit the play?" I asked.

"I'm not going to compete with you for Kyle," Chloe said.

"But that has nothing to do with the play."

Chloe's eyes widened. "It has everything to do with it."

I knew it was my turn to spill the beans. "All Kyle and I did was talk. I mean, I think he likes to talk to me, and I like to listen because I have a crush on him. He needs encouragement, Chloe.

He wanted someone to watch his knee operation, so I watched it."

"I saw you kiss," Chloe said.

"You saw me kissing Kyle," I said. "It was sort of impulsive. I think he was just as surprised as you. Believe me, Chloe, there's really nothing going on between us. I wish there was, but there isn't."

"That makes two of us," Chloe said with a sigh.

I glanced at her. "Can I ask what the story is?"

Chloe raised her hands and let them fall. "We really liked each other once. Maybe it was even love. Then . . . I don't know."

"He hurt his knee?"

"It started to change before that," she said. "I think we both felt like we were supposed to be together. Like everyone expected it. I think we forgot why we'd gotten together in the first place."

"Do you remember now?" I asked.

Chloe suddenly smiled. "Oh, come on, Bo. He's a hunk, why else?"

"Are you serious?"

"Half-serious. It's not only because he was handsome and on the football team. He was funny and sweet, too."

"And no competition for you academically," I guessed.

"Right. But now . . . it's like a doll you cherish, but don't want to play with anymore." She turned to me quickly. "Promise you won't quote me."

"I won't . . . But you can't keep him on a shelf."

"I know."

"Everyone wants you to come back to the play," I said. "Including me."

"Why?"

"God, Chloe, do you have to ask?"

"I thought I was a big pain. I'm obnoxious and demanding and by opening night everyone hates me."

"True. Is that why you never come to cast parties?"

I took her silence as an affirmation.

"Well, I'll let you in on a secret," I said. "You make us look better than we are, and deep down after we all get finished hating you, we appreciate it."

"And what about Kyle?" she asked.

"Your guess is as good as mine."

KYLE

It gets hot under the lights. You sweat. It's not just the heat. It's nerves. They were all out there: the Pinheads, Mr. Orillio, your dad, your stepmom, even IT, sitting in Jackie's lap chewing on his rag because Bo's the stage manager and Jackie wouldn't trust any other baby-sitter with him.

So you do your best and you mangle a line here and there, but you know the story so well that you can talk your way through each flub and get back on track. It's kind of like holding a one-point lead with five minutes to go. If you can just get through it, if you just don't do anything really stupid, you'll be okay.

Then it's over, and somehow you did it. The curtain goes down and for the first time in an hour and a half, the audience can't see you. You take a deep breath and want to shout or scream or tear off your clothes and run around naked, but you have to do one last thing first.

BO

The curtain had just come down. The actors and actresses were wandering around backstage with dazed expressions, and every time they intersected with another actor they'd hug, even though normally they might have hated each other's guts.

"It wasn't half-bad," Ben McGillis muttered and walked around in circles. "Not half-bad."

Alice trudged toward me with her head bowed. "I was awful."

"You were the best." I hugged her.

"You're just saying that."

"You're the only one among us with even a remote chance of a future in this business."

"You really mean it?" She looked up and actually smiled.

"Cross my heart and hope to die." Over her shoulder I watched Kyle and Chloe exchange awkward little smiles. They didn't say anything to each other. They didn't hug. After a brief, uncomfortable moment, they both turned away.

That was over, too.

"Bows, everyone!" Mr. Goodrich whispered hoarsely.

From my spot in the wings I watched them all line up. For a lot of them, it was the last curtain call of their high school careers, maybe their last curtain call ever.

The curtain went up and the crowd started clapping and cheering. Kyle, Chloe, Alice, and the others stood out there in the spotlights, basking in the adulation. Then Alice and Howie Tardibono ran offstage and dragged Mr. Goodrich out and the cheering surged again. They all deserved it. They'd all worked incredibly hard.

Then Chloe backed out of the line and hurried toward me.

"Get back out there!" I whispered, waving her back. "They're still applauding."

"I know." Chloe grabbed my wrist, then started to pull.

"What are you doing!?" I gasped.

"Getting you what you deserve," she said, pulling me out toward the stage.

I pulled back. "You're crazy! I can't! I'm dressed like a janitor. My hair's not even brushed!"

"Go on, Bo," Bobby said, joining Chloe and

pushing from behind.

Suddenly I was standing in the glare of the lights, facing the crowd. Chloe was still holding my wrist.

"Our stage manager!" she shouted to the audience.

The applause surged. And what was really sweet was that Mr. Goodrich and the actors and actresses all turned and applauded, too.

For that one moment, they were all cheering . . . for me.

Finally.

KYLE

After the show I came out of the greenroom and found Eddie in the hall.

"Pretty good, bro." He held up his hand for a high five.

"You were out there?" I asked, surprised.

"Sure, why not?" He started to chew on his thumb. "Look, Kyle, about what I said the other day—"

"Hey, don't sweat it." I patted him on the shoulder. "I know how you felt. You had a right to be pissed."

Eddie gave me a curious look. "So, you gonna make a career of this?"

"Nah, it was just something to do."

"What're you gonna do next?"

"Go to the cast party. Want to come?"

"That's not what I meant," Eddie said as we started down the hall. "What I meant was—"

"I know what you meant," I cut him off. "I

guess the first thing I'm gonna do is get off Mr. Orillio's most-likely-to-screw-up list. After that, I'm open for suggestions."

"Maybe we could get into something together," Eddie said. "Like plan something for this spring."

"Sounds good."

BO

Kyle brought his friend Eddie to the cast party at Bobby's house and they sat around in the kitchen talking about sports. I waited until Eddie went to the bathroom and then went up to Kyle.

"Can we talk?" I asked.

"Uh, okay."

"Not here," I said. "Let's go outside."

We went out the sliding glass doors to the patio. It was cold and dark and our breaths curled up in white plumes in the moonlight.

"I guess you know how I feel," I said.

He nodded and didn't say anything. I'd been praying it would be different, that he'd sweep me into his arms and tell me he loved me now and forever. But reality set in. I can't say I was surprised.

"I guess I know how you feel," I said.

"It's not you, Bo," he said. "I mean, I've been with Chloe for so long. I'm still trying to figure it all out."

"Maybe once you've had some time . . ." I hated myself for saying it, but hope springs eternal.

"Maybe." Kyle tried to smile, but he knew and I knew it wasn't to be.

For a second I thought I'd burst into tears.

But then I got hold of myself.

Like Alice says, they're just guys.

◇ ◇ ◇

Chloe didn't come to the cast party, so I got Kyle's friend Eddie to give me a ride to her house. Eddie isn't quite as tall as Kyle and his shoulders aren't as broad. To be honest, he isn't as handsome, but he certainly is good-looking. And he has a nice smile.

"You're the stage manager, right?" he said as he drove.

"I was. Now that the play's over, I'm just Bo. You're the quarterback."

"I was. Now that the season's over, I'm just Eddie."

We smiled at each other.

When you think about it, it's really amazing how many similarities there are between quarter-backing and stage-managing. You both basically run the team.

"Here we are," he said, pulling into her drive-way.

"Thanks for the ride," I said and started to get out.

"Uh, Bo?" Eddie said.

"Yes?"

"Think you'll be back at the cast party later?"

"I don't know."

Eddie looked a little disappointed.

"But if I'm not, I'll see you at school," I added.

Eddie smiled. "Great."

I went up the walk and rang the bell. Chloe answered the door holding the portable phone to her ear. She looked surprised.

"Bo, why aren't you at the cast party?"

"I wanted to see you."

"Hold on a second." She turned away and finished her phone conversation. "You'll never guess who that was."

"Who?"

"Morgan Landon. He directs the community theater."

"Really?"

"He was in the audience tonight. He just called to tell me they're doing *Bye-Bye Birdie* this spring. He wants me to try out."

"Serious?" I gasped.

Chloe nodded and her eyes sparkled with excitement.

"Hey, wait a minute," I said. "Lots of people try out for those parts. They get college kids, even semiprofessional actors. You'll be up against some real talent."

"So?"

"Competition, remember?" I said.

"I'll try if you'll try," Chloe said.

"Me, act?"

"No, silly. Assistant stage manager."

"Assistant stage manager for the community theater," I mumbled. "I like the sound of that."

"Got the playbook?"

"Somewhere in my room," I said.

"Let's go get it."

"Now?"

"Sure. Why not? And then we'll go out for no-fat frozen yogurt."

"Fabulous," I said, then hesitated. "Only . . ."

"What's wrong?" Chloe asked.

"Alice. I really think she should try out for the play, too."

"Okay, just as long as she and I agree not to try out for the same part," Chloe said.

"Deal." We headed for her car. The future looked rosy, exciting and unpredictable.

K Y L E

Jake was up half the night crying. Around 3 a.m. I think I heard Jackie say something about him cutting molars, but I could've been dreaming. This morning I got up and went into the kitchen. Jake was sitting in his high chair, sucking on a bottle. Jackie was standing at the kitchen counter making a cup of coffee. She was wearing her pink robe with a big white stain of baby cheese on the shoulder. Her hair was snarled and uncombed, her eyes looked puffy and ringed.

"Want some breakfast, Kyle?" she asked.

"I'll get it," I said. I mean, it doesn't take a lot of work to pour a glass of orange juice and a bowl of Cheerios.

I sat down at the table to eat. Jackie leaned against the counter and sipped her coffee. Nobody said anything. The only sound was Jake sucking on his bottle. It was like we were wax figures in a museum, except we were all moving.

Then there was this crash. I turned around, but all I saw was steaming coffee all over the floor, and pieces of the glass coffee pot all over the counter. Jackie looked like she was in shock.

"You okay?" I asked. I didn't see any cuts or anything.

Jackie's eyes filled with tears. The next thing I knew she turned and ran out of the kitchen. I heard the bedroom door slam. Jake was still sucking happily on his bottle like life was normal. I don't know what Jackie expected when she married my father and moved in with us. But I bet it wasn't this.

Jake finished his bottle and chucked it onto the floor. I picked it up and put it on the counter. I had ten minutes left before I had to leave for school so I picked up the broken glass and mopped up the coffee with paper towels. I put the dirty dishes in the dishwasher.

Then I noticed Jake's face was red and he was bearing down pretty hard in the high chair.

Great timing, kid.

Jackie still hadn't come out of the bedroom.

Jake finished his business and gave me a big grin. You're not going to do it, I told myself.

Jake just sat there happy as a clam. What does a one-and-a-half-year-old know?

"Okay, Jake," I said, and lifted him out of the high chair. I carried him into the nursery and got him to lie down on the changing table. I used about a hundred baby wipes.

Then it was time to put on the new diaper.

I know it's one of those things that must be incredibly obvious to anyone who does it often, but I just couldn't quite figure out how it went.

"Kyle! What are you doing?" Next thing I knew, Jackie rushed to the changing table, like maybe she thought I was going to dissect the kid or something. She looked at Jake and saw that I'd cleaned him up. Filled with surprise, she turned to me. Our eyes met for a second and then I looked away.

"Here's what you do," she said, taking the diaper and putting it on Jake. It looked pretty easy once I saw how it was done. I just hoped Jackie wouldn't say anything embarrassing.

"Guess I better get to school," I said.

"Sure, Kyle," Jackie said. But she smiled.

BO

Today I stood before the Honorable Justice Paul Topal in county court.

"Would you please tell the court why you have petitioned to change your name?" he asked.

"How would you like to have a daughter named Bo Vine, Your Honor?" I replied.

The honorable justice frowned and looked down at his papers. "Petition approved," he said.

Back home, I broke the news to my mother. When it comes to things like changing your name, it's always best to do it first and tell your parents about it later. That way they can totally freak, but it's too late to do anything.

"Mom," I said, handing her the petition approved by the Honorable Justice Topal. "I've changed my name. It's legal and everything."

Her eyebrows went up. "You're serious?"

"To Delia, but I want everyone to call me Dee."

My mother read the petition and then looked up at me. "Dee Vine?" she said. Then she actually smiled.

◇　◇　◇

Life is mysterious. Who knows why we fall in love with who we fall in love with, or what we can and can't do if we put our minds to it. If I've learned one thing from all this, it's never to put limits on myself again. You have to try new things. You can hate failure, but you mustn't let the fear of it paralyze you. Like the poet said, "Tis better to have loved and lost than never to have loved at all."

Don't be afraid to try.

Don't be afraid to fail.

Don't be afraid to color your hair.

Try to understand where people are coming from.

Don't forget that most people are really good at heart.

And if you hate your name, change it.

Todd Strasser is the author of more than seventy novels for young people. He started to write seriously when he was twenty-two. At that time he worked for a newspaper. Later he sold his first novel and used the money from the book to start a fortune cookie company.

The idea for *How I Changed My Life* grew out of several different personal experiences. In college Todd became involved with an actress and, as a result, spent a lot of time around theatrical productions. Later, he suffered a serious injury to his knee that dashed any hopes for a career in professional sports.